VOODOO VIPER

The living nightmare slid slowly toward the man in black, its dark, obsidian eyes reflecting its soul-less nature.

Henri Pétion performed a sweeping, obsequious bow. "Lord Damballah, I am yours to command! Do with me as you will." He straightened, his arms at his sides.

The Snake God acknowledged the request.

Suddenly sweeping forward, the black serpent's enormous head darted at the expectant human, its maw opening wide enough to accommodate a horse. Exhibiting lightning rapidity, striking before Pétion could utter a single sound, the snake snapped its mouth shut over its prey, then reared back.

Blade felt revulsion at the ghastly sight. He could see Pétion's ankles and feet jutting from between the reptile's lips, the black shoes kicking and twisting, and then the snake tilted its head upward, gulped, and swallowed.

Pétion's feet disappeared.

Other books in the *Endworld* series:

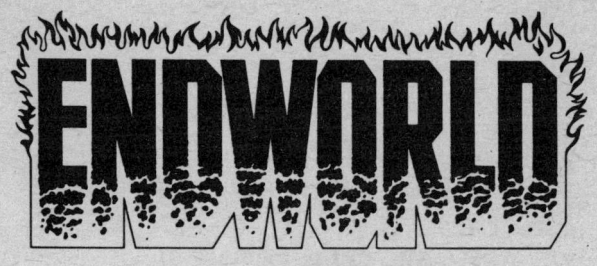

ENDWORLD

#24:
NEW ORLEANS RUN
DAVID ROBBINS

LEISURE BOOKS   **L**   NEW YORK CITY

Dedicated to . . .
Judy, Joshua, and Shane.

And to the memory of
Robert E. Howard.

A LEISURE BOOK®

January 1991

Published by

Dorchester Publishing Co., Inc.
276 Fifth Avenue
New York, NY 10001

Printed in the United States of America.

PROLOGUE

The young woman halted and spun, her long raven tresses swirling, and stared intently at the benighted landscape to her rear. "I think we're being followed," she asserted.

"You're imagining things," her companion stated. A brown-haired man in his early twenties, he wore faded jeans, a green shirt, and a denim backpack.

"Didn't you hear something just now?" the woman asked anxiously. She wore dark blue pants and a matching blouse. Her green eyes narrowed as she tried to pierce the gloom.

"No."

"I did."

The man turned and surveyed the rolling expanse of open field they had just traversed. Scant illumination was provided by the quarter moon already several hours high, but he could see well enough to ascertain no one trailed them. "As usual, your nerves are getting the better of you. We're not being followed."

"My nerves are fine, thank you."

"Come on, Eleanore. You know you become jumpy as hell when we make these trips."

Eleanore made no comment. Instead, she turned and resumed hiking to the west, her spine rigid, her fists clenched at her sides.

"In one of your moods again, I see," the man remarked as he followed.

"Don't start, Jerry."

"I'm only mentioning the obvious."

"Obvious to you maybe."

Jerry sighed and adjusted the tight straps on the backpack. "I wish you'd quit looking down your nose at me, Ms. High and Mighty. We're both part of the Resistance, you know. Your family may have been wealthy and powerful decades ago, way back before World War Three, but you're no better than the rest of us poor white trash now."

Again Eleanore stopped, and this time she fixed a flashing glare on her surprised companion. "Is that what you and the others think? That I have some kind of snobbish attitude?"

A noncommittal shrug was Jerry's reply.

"Answer me, damn you!"

"Let's keep going," Jerry said, starting to walk past her. "This is hardly the proper time or place to air our gripes."

Eleanore grabbed his left wrist and held fast. "What's wrong with right now? We're in the middle of nowhere, four miles from New Orleans. No one can hear us. The *tonton macoutes* have no idea we're here. So let's get this off our chests."

"Be serious," Jerry stated testily, trying to pull his arm loose. "The eyes and ears of Damballah are everywhere."

"Don't give me that garbage," Eleanore snapped.

"You never know," Jerry noted, and ceased tugging. "Look, will you quit behaving like a five-year-old and let go of me? Adrien is waiting for us."

"We're ahead of schedule," Eleanor pointed out. "A few minutes won't hurt."

"No."

"Please," Eleanore pleaded. "Ever since I joined the Resistance four months ago, everyone except Violet and Rad has been giving me the cold shoulder. At first I thought it was all in my head, but lately I've come to realize that none of you like me. Why?''

"You don't want to know," Jerry said.

"Then it's true," Eleanore said softly. She released his wrist and gazed absently at the flickering lights in the city to the east. "I can hardly believe it. What did I ever do to any of you?''

"Nothing," Jerry admitted, fidgeting uncomfortably.

"Then why?''

A strained silence persisted for all of ten seconds, until Jerry took a deep breath and blurted out, "Because no one trusts you, that's why.''

Eleanore looked at him in astonishment. "No one trusts me? I'm as dedicated to the cause as anyone else. And I have more to lose by joining the Resistance than most. So why doesn't anyone trust me?''

"Some suspect you might be a plant, a spy.''

"A spy!" Eleanore exclaimed angrily.

"Shhhhh!" Jerry cautioned. "Keep the noise down. We don't want anyone to hear us.''

"You're the one who claims no one is following us," Eleanore reminded him. "And the nearest house is two miles away. So who could hear us?''

"You never know.''

"Is that your favorite phrase or something?" Eleanore inquired, and then continued before he could answer. "To tell you the truth, I don't much care who hears me. You've handed me the worst insult possible and I demand to know the reason.''

"You're no dummy. Surely you can figure it all out by yourself.''

"Tell me, damn you!" Eleanore insisted, a shrill tinge to her tone.

Jerry placed his hands on his hips and regarded her critically. "All right. But remember you asked for it." He paused. "We all know you're Violet's friend, but how can you blame us for suspecting you? You were one of Laveau's women, for crying out loud. You lived in the lap of luxury. Fine food, fine clothes—anything you wanted, you got. And there were always dozens of slaves waiting to serve you at any time of the day or night. How can you expect any sane person to believe you'd give all of that up to join the Resistance?''

"You're right. I was one of Laveau's women. Was. Past tense. As in past history. But the son of a bitch dumped me, just like he does every woman once she turns nineteen. Surely you know he only beds sweet young things,'' Eleanore stated, saying the last three words bitterly.

"There's a rumor to that effect,'' Jerry acknowledged.

"It's no lousy rumor,'' Eleanore snapped. "Laveau is the most superstitious bastard on the planet. He won't eat food that has been touched by anything metal. All of the cooking utensils at his estate, all of the pots and pans, the forks, spoons, and knives are made of wood. All of his clothes, all of the washcloths and towels are red because only red fabric can touch his body. And five times a day he has to drink fresh goat's blood.''

"Goat's blood?'' Jerry said distastefully.

"That's right. He firmly believes that if he breaks any of those rules, plus dozens of others, his magic will grow weak and his enemies will be able to defeat him.''

"And that's why he dumped you?''

"Yep. He'll only have sex with women between fifteen and nineteen.''

"A fifteen-year-old is hardly a woman,'' Jerry mentioned with evident scorn.

"They are by the time Laveau gets through with them,'' Eleanore remarked, her voice suddenly raspy. "I should know. I went through the whole routine. The *tonton macoutes* showed up at my parents' house when I was one month shy of my fifteenth birthday and informed them Laveau wanted me as one of his harem. They went on and on about the honor I was receiving, and they paid my parents twenty pieces of gold in compensation.''

"Did your folks accept?''

"Of course.''

Jerry recoiled in shock. "How could they sell their own daughter to that fiend?''

"Be realistic. What choice did they have? If they'd refused, the *tonton macoutes* would have taken me anyway and about a week later my mom and dad would have mysteriously disappeared,'' Eleanore said, and bowed her head. "So they did what they had to do. On my fifteenth birthday, which most girls celebrate with their family, and maybe with a boyfriend on hand, I was carried kicking and screaming from our house and taken into the bayou to Laveau's estate. That very night he took me for the first time.'' She paused and inhaled deeply.

"There's no need to go on,'' Jerry advised her.

"I want you to know the truth,'' Eleanore declared, glancing at him. "I want you to tell the others in the Resistance so they'll understand the reason I joined. I'm not a damned spy. I want to make the Baron pay for what he did to me.''

"Revenge is your motive,'' Jerry said.

"Can you think of a better one?''

"Yes.''

"You can?'' Eleanore queried in surprise.

"Freedom.''

"I believe in freedom.''

"Perhaps you do,'' Jerry responded. "But you're more interested in getting revenge for the indignities you suffered.''

"Indignities, hell! I went through sheer torture!''

"Okay. Granted. But freedom is a secondary consideration for you. For me, and for most of us in the Resistance, freedom is our motivation for opposing the rule of Damballah, freedom for the thousands of people who live in daily fear of the Baron, of Majesta, of the *tonton macoutes* and all the rest. New Orleans has been under the sway of evil for far too long. I want my children to be able to walk down the street in safety."

"Do you have kids? I didn't know that."

"Not yet. But one day I'll meet the right woman, and then—who knows?"

"I hope you do," Eleanore offered sincerely.

"Thanks." Jerry turned to the west. "Look, we'd really best get our butts in gear. I know there's plenty of time until daylight, but I don't like cutting the margin too close. Let's deliver the goods to Adrien and get back."

"Are you sure you're not just scared of the dark?" Eleanore joked, breaking into a brisk stride. "Are you afraid Damballah will get you?" She laughed at the notion.

Jerry walked on her right. "Don't mock Damballah."

"What's with you? You act as if you believe in the nonsense they spout about the thing."

"I do."

Eleanore broke stride for an instant, then caught up with him. "And here I had you pegged as a sensible guy."

"Make fun of me all you want, but I know what I saw."

"You saw it?" Eleanore questioned in amazement.

"Yep."

"You're putting me on. I mean, in all the years I was at Laveau's estate I never saw it. Granted, they wouldn't let me or any of the other women in his stable anywhere near the *houmfor,* but if the thing was real you'd think I'd have caught a glimpse of it."

Jerry looked at her and found himself admiring the fine lines of her lovely features. "My brother and I saw it about twelve years ago."

"Tell me," she urged.

"Well, we'd gone into the bayou in my dad's canoe to do some fishing. We weren't supposed to go by ourselves, but you know how kids can be. Anyway, we stayed out later than we intended, and by the time we started back the sun was setting. Our arms grew tired and we pulled in next to this small island to rest." He quit speaking and scoured the ground ahead, searching the waist-high weeds for the faint trace of the trail.

"Go on. What happened next?"

"We heard this strange noise, like a loud hissing, and we were stunned to see this enormous creature moving through the water to the south of us. We froze, which is probably just as well. If that thing had spotted us, we would have been its supper."

Eleanore could detect a vestige of terror in his voice even after so many years, and she inadvertently shuddered as she imagined the harrowing experience he'd undergone. "What did it look like?"

"Exactly as the legend states."

"Dear God."

"The Lord has no connection to that monster. Damballah is straight from hell."

A horrifying thought occurred to Eleanore and she glanced around them in consternation. "What if we bump into it?"

Jerry patted the survival knife attached to his belt above his right hip. "I'd do my best to protect you. Your best bet, though, would be to run. I couldn't hold something that size off for very long."

Suddenly the night seemed to be shrouded by a sinister veil, and lurking in every shadow was a bloodthirsty creature or a demon from the inferno. Eleanore moved closer to Jerry. "How soon will we be at the cabin?"

"About five minutes."

"Good," Eleanore said, and that single word was pregnant with expectation and relief. She listened to the myriad of sounds characteristic of a typical muggy Louisiana night in early October; the chirping and buzzing of insects, the croaking of bullfrogs, the peculiar bellowing of gators from the swamp to the south, the hooting of owls, the occasional fluttering of bats from overhead, and, of course, the distinct roars and eerie cries of the mutations. "I never realized how isolated we are out here," she commented.

"Where else could the Resistance operate the radio?" Jerry replied. "Ever since the great flood, the bayou has pretty much taken over all of the land encircling New Orleans. This thirty-acre tract is one of the largest dry sections for miles."

"I've been meaning to ask. Where did the Resistance obtain the shortwave radio anyway?"

"About five months ago Rad was poking through those abandoned buildings on Canal Street. He stumbled across, of all things, a sub-basement in one of the old department stores. In it, sitting on a dusty table, was the shortwave and other gear."

"Rad took a big risk," Eleanore noted. "The *tonton macoutes* have declared those buildings off-limits."

"They can't be everywhere at once."

Eleanore pondered for a moment. "I was told those scum have gone all through those buildings, from top to bottom, many times. How could they have missed the radio?"

"Easy. Rad found it quite by accident. He saw a fat rat and tried to bag it with his slingshot, but the rodent ran behind a pile of debris. When Rad looked, he found a narrow opening in the wall at floor level, a concealed maintenance shaft to the ventilation system. He crawled in, wiggled along the passages, and came to the room containing the shortwave. It must have belonged to an ancient maintainence worker. Maybe he put it there to listen to while he was on his breaks, or maybe he had a friend he liked to contact on a regular basis. For all we know, he could have stolen it from the department store."

"You certainly know a lot about the prewar life-style," Eleanore observed.

"I've ready every book I can find on the subject."

"Didn't the *tonton macoutes* burn all the libraries to the ground?"

"Yeah, but they weren't able to collect every book in New Orleans. The Resistance has collected a couple of hundred over the years, and they're all stored in a safe place."

"I didn't know the Resistance has its own library."

"It's one of our best-kept secrets. Only the inner circle knows the exact location. You have to be with the Resistance for a year or so before you'll be allowed to go there," Jerry related.

"There you go again. It certainly is nice to know that everyone has such confidence in me."

Jerry looked at her. "Don't take it personally. I wasn't permitted to visit the library until I'd been with the Resistance eleven months."

"Really."

Jerry nodded. "Some of the books are priceless. There are several on the prewar society. One tells all about how to live off the land. And another one describes how to build a boat from scratch. If we could locate the materials, if we could build the boat without the *tonton macoutes* finding out, then if worse came to worst we could head for the Gulf."

"That's a lot of ifs," Eleanore remarked.

"It's just one of the ideas we're working on in case we can't raise anyone on the shortwave radio."

"Has Adrien had any luck yet?"

"No," Jerry replied. "He's been broadcasting every night for two weeks, and so far he hasn't received an answer." He gazed thoughtfully at the star-filled night. "There must be someone out there who can hear us, who can help."

"I hope you're right. But for all we know the rest of the country could be in the same shape as New Orleans," Eleanore mentioned.

"Then we're all as good as dead."

They tramped through the weeds for another two minutes without speaking.

"Hey," Eleanore said, breaking the silence. "Something just occurred to me. If the Resistance has had the shortwave for five months, why has Adrien only been broadcasting for two weeks?"

"First we had to discover a safe place to broadcast from," Jerry answered. "We also had to dig up some batteries to power the unit. That alone took us three months, until we came across a stash in a demolished hardware store. And we had to figure out how to use the thing. Unfortunately, the radio didn't come with a set of instructions. You've seen all the dials and switches it has.''

"Yes," Eleanore said. "This is my third trip out here, remember?"

"And we'll keep bringing him supplies and checking on his progress every four or five days until he makes contact," Jerry stated.

"Why doesn't he just come into the city for his provisions?"

"Because we don't want the shortwave left alone."

"Then send someone out here to stay with him," Eleanore proposed.

"What difference does it make? Violet set up the arrangements, and they're fine as far as I'm concerned."

"Oh. Well, she knows best."

"How long have you known her anyway?" Jerry inquired.

"Violet and I go way back," Eleanore divulged. "We've been friends since we were six years old. Her folks lived next door to my parents for years until they moved to the French Quarter."

"I was raised in Algiers."

Eleanore studied his profile for a moment. "Algiers is one of the roughest sections of New Orleans."

"I got by okay. We lived on the south end, and it was easy for my brother and me to slip away to Bayou Segnette whenever we wanted."

"You talk so fondly of your brother. Where is he now?"

"Dead."

"Oh. I'm sorry."

"He died three and a half years ago."

"What happened?"

"The *tonton macoutes* caught him returning from a hunting trip with a rifle. The gun had been in our family since before I was born. We'd kept it hidden under the floorboards and only used it on special occasions to conserve the ammunition.

Howie took it out to go bag a deer. He wanted to treat my father and mother to venison steak for their anniversary," Jerry detailed.

"You don't need to tell me the rest. I know possessing a firearm is strictly forbidden, and I can imagine what they did to him."

"No, you can't. They pulled his toenails out with a pair of pliers, peeled the skin from his body, and then boiled him alive in salt water," Jerry disclosed, his voice wavering.

"Did the bastards make your family watch?"

"No, but they bragged about it afterwards. And they told us that they chopped up Howie's body and fed the bits and pieces to the alligators in the swamp surrounding the Baron's estate."

"So I'm not the only one who joined the Resistance to get a little revenge," Eleanore deduced.

"No, I guess not. But I've changed since I joined. Violet has helped me to realize that freedom for all is a higher cause to serve than personal revenge," Jerry said. He spotted the cabin dead ahead, a solitary light glowing in the north window, and pointed. "Look."

"It's about time."

They quickened their pace, and in short order drew within ten yards of the closed front door.

"Strange," Jerry commented.

"What is?"

"Adrien knows better than to leave the window uncovered. That lantern light can be seen for miles."

"Then why didn't we see it sooner?"

The question prompted Jerry to abruptly halt. He scrutinized the dilapidated structure warily and strained his ears to detect sounds from within. All was quiet.

"What's the matter?" Eleanore inquired.

"I'm not sure. Stay put," Jerry advised, and walked toward the wooden door, his right hand on his survival knife.

Eleanore glanced around apprehensively. She realized the insects in their immediate vicinity had ceased making noise.

"I don't like this, Jerry."

"Me neither."

"Let's get out of here."

"Not until we check on Adrien," Jerry responded, and called out. "Adrien! Are you in there?"

The front door unexpectedly opened and out strode a tall, thin man dressed all in red, his flared Afro adding inches to his height. At the same time, from every direction, dozens of men dressed all in black converged on the cabin.

Eleanore took one look at the figure in red and gasped in terror. "Baron Laveau!"

CHAPTER ONE

He ran to the east with startling speed, as well he should considering he was a hybrid of human and feline traits, a genetically engineered being who possessed human and bestial features in equal measure, a cat-man endowed with extraordinary strength and agility. Except for a gray loincloth, his four-foot frame lacked clothing. But he wasn't exactly naked because his entire body sported a thick coat of short, grayish-brown fur. Tapered nails capped his bony fingers. His ears, like a cat's, were pointed. And his face, decidedly feline in aspect, contained a pair of slanted, vivid green eyes.

Ahead of him rose a hill.

He grinned in anticipation, knowing they would be there, and loped up the narrow trail to the summit. True to his prediction, he found them seated on the east rim. "Hey, you turkeys! Guess what?"

The pair enjoying the sunshine and the tranquility turned at the sound of the newcomer's raspy voice, and both, oddly, scowled.

On the right sat another hybrid, a creature who strongly

resembled a two-legged ferret. Like the cat-man, he was only four feet in height, and his weight came to a mere 60 pounds. Brown hair, about three inches long, covered his whole form. Also like the cat-man, he wore a loincloth, only his was black. His head was oversized for his slight build, and from the front of it protruded a long nose that nearly resembled a snout. His brown eyes narrowed as he regarded the cat-man critically.

So did the other creature. Five feet ten and quite humanoid in aspect, this being wore a brown loincloth. His gray skin was leathery, his visage hawklike, his nose pointed almost like a beak. A thin slit of a mouth, tiny circles of flesh for ears, and bizarre eyes with bright red pupils lent him an alien appearance.

The cat-man came to a halt a few feet from the duo and glanced expectantly from one to the other. "Didn't you bozos hear me?"

"We heard you, Lynx," said the ferret-man.

"Unfortunately, yes?" added the other.

Lynx placed his hands on his hips and exhaled loudly. "I boogied all the way out here to bring you the good news and this is the way you treat me?"

The ferret-man looked at the humanoid. "Did he say *good* news?"

"We are definitely in trouble, no?" responded the other.

A muted hiss issued from Lynx's thin lips. "I go to all this trouble, and you two act like jerks."

"Would you do us a favor?" the ferret-man asked.

"Sure, Ferret," Lynx replied, brightening. "You know I'd do anything for you guys."

"Then would you go jump in the moat and see if you can stay under for an hour or so?"

The humanoid cackled.

"You think that's funny, do you, Gremlin?" Lynx demanded.

"Quite humorous, yes?" Gremlin replied, and chuckled.

"Look, do you want to hear the good news or not?" Lynx snapped.

"We pass," Ferret said.

"You'll be sorry," Lynx told them. "This is a once-in-a-blue-moon opportunity for us."

"We still pass," Ferret reiterated.

"Trust me. You'll like it," Lynx asserted.

"Trust *you*?" Ferret almost exploded, rising and taking a step toward the cat-man. "Every time you say that, we wind up in more trouble than we can handle."

"You're exaggerating," Lynx said.

Ferret looked at Gremlin. "Am I?"

"Not exaggerating, no," Gremlin answered, standing slowly. "Understatement, yes?"

"Okay! Fine!" Lynx declared, and folded his wiry arms across his chest. "Be this way! If you don't want to hear my good news, then I'm not going to tell you."

"Thank you," Ferret said, and turned to Gremlin. "What do you say we go grab a bite to eat?"

"Fine by Gremlin."

"Samson told me we could stop by his cabin for supper," Ferret mentioned, leading the way to the west.

Lynx leaped in front of them to block their path. "Forget about food for a minute! This is more important."

"I thought you weren't going to tell us," Ferret noted.

"I figure secretly you both want to know."

"You're wrong," Ferret said. He pressed his hands over his ears and deliberately turned his back to the cat-man.

"Go ahead. Act like a dork," Lynx said. "But I know you can hear me, so listen to this." He paused for dramatic effect. "Blade has agreed to take us on the next mission. We leave first thing in the morning!"

Gremlin seemed to transform into stone, his mouth hanging wide open.

Ferret's arms dropped and he whirled, anger contorting his feral features. "What?"

"Isn't it terrific?" Lynx beamed. "I finally persuaded the big dummy to take us along. And you'll never guess where we're going."

"I don't want to go anywhere," Ferret said.

"You'll change your mind when you hear the great news," Lynx assured him.

"I don't want to hear it."

"Yes, you do. You only think you don't."

"Don't tell me or I'll rip your face off."

"New Orleans."

Ferret's slim shoulders drooped and he raised his eyes to the heavens. "Why me? Why is it always me?"

"Don't forget me, yes?" Gremlin interjected.

"What's wrong with you guys?" Lynx said excitedly. "This is fantastic! We finally get to leave the Home on a run. Aren't you excited?"

"In a word, no," Ferret said.

"Why not? Look at how long we've been cooped up here, walkin' the ramparts on guard duty, playin' nursemaid to the Family, huntin' game, and generally being bored to tears. Now we'll see a little action."

Ferret's temper became several degrees hotter. "A little action? You moron! A little action could get us all killed."

"Do I take it you're upset?"

"I'll show you upset," Ferret growled, and wagged his right fist.

Lynx backed up a step and smiled. "You just need time to adjust to the idea. Then you'll see that I'm right, as usual."

"Right? You?" Ferret snorted contemptuously.

"Where am I off base then?"

"Between the ears," Ferret retorted, and then launched into a diatribe, scarcely able to control his simmering indignation. "First of all, you dipstick, it's impossible to be 'cooped up' in a thirty-acre compound. Second of all, Gremlin and I like pulling guard duty on the walls. We like hunting game for the Family. We have no desire to see any action whatsoever. The more peaceful our lives are, the better we like it."

"But you're Warriors," Lynx said.

"And whose fault is that?" Ferret asked. "*You* were the one who wanted to become a Warrior, remember? *You* were the one who talked Blade and Hickok into sponsoring us for Warrior status. And you're the one who wants to go on a run outside of the Home, not us."

"Does this mean you don't like the idea?"

"It sucks!"

"What, exactly, don't you like about it?"

Ferret's lips compressed and he seemed about to leap upon his friend. Instead, he stormed to the west without another word.

"Pitiful," Lynx muttered, hastening after him.

"Pitiful, yes?" Gremlin commented, shaking his head as he followed.

The cat-man easily caught up with Ferret and tried to grab his wrist.

"Touch me and you die."

"Boy, are you a grump or what?"

"I was doing just fine until you showed up," Ferret said testily.

"Would you stand still and let me talk to you?" Lynx asked.

"No."

"A minute. All I ask is a minute of your time."

"Go suck on a live hand grenade."

Exasperated, Lynx suddenly ran several yards in front of Ferret and halted directly in front of him, forcing Ferret to stop or go around.

Ferret halted.

"Good. Now we can discuss this like intelligent hybrids," the cat-man declared.

"Get your face out of my life."

"Calm down. Hear me out, please."

"I'll count to three," Ferret stated.

"Look, is it too much of an imposition for you to listen

to what I have to say? Listen. That's all. And if you still don't want to go on the run, then I'll personally go to Blade and tell him to pick another Triad. What do you say?''

"You will?'' Ferret asked suspiciously.

"My word of honor.''

"Put it in writing.''

"Give me a break,'' Lynx said. "I'm trying to be fair about this. I don't want the two of you to do something you don't want to do.''

Ferret glanced at Gremlin, who stood on his right. "What do you think?''

"Where Lynx is concerned, Gremlin never think, no,'' the humanoid said.

"Come on, guys! How many years have we been best buddies? Six? Seven? Do you really think I would do anything that didn't have your best interests at heart?''

"Yes,'' Ferret stated flatly.

"Okay. So maybe once or twice I've let my enthusiasm get the better of me, but this time it's different. This time I'm tryin' to fulfill our biological imperative.''

"You're what?'' Ferret blurted out in astonishment. "Where did you ever learn big words like those?''

"He's been reading the dictionary again, yes?'' Gremlin speculated.

"Dictionary, hell. I'm not as dumb as most everybody seems to think I am. And I know there are certain facts we have to accept and live by accordingly. Fact number one is that we were created by the lousy Doktor to be members of his Genetic Research Division, to be part of his private assassin corps. We were bred in a test tube to be fighters. The perfect killers. That's what we are. And all the wishful thinkin' in the world won't change our past or make us anything else.''

"He hasn't been reading a dictionary,'' Ferret cracked. "He's been browsing through the philosophy books in the Family library.''

Lynx frowned. "Will you glue your mouth shut until I'm

done? This is serious business. For almost two years now we've been Warriors. And as I was tryin' to explain before, for two years all we've done is guard the walls and hunt game. Big friggin' deal. We weren't brought into existence to be bored to tears. We were created for action. We're genetically engineered mutations, damn it! We're different from everyone and everything else on the whole planet. The Doktor went to all the trouble of takin' ordinary human embryos and addin' animal traits for a reason.''

"Yeah. So we could go out and get our heads shot off protecting his sorry ass," Ferret snapped.

"Bingo."

"What?"

"You've just hit the nail on the head. Our whole purpose for being is to be gladiators.''

"Gladiators?" Ferret declared, his eyebrows arching. He glanced at Gremlin. "Did he say gladiators?"

"I picked up the word from Spartacus and it fits us to a T. He told me all about how those ancient Roman dudes were trained to go out in an arena and kick butt. We're the same way. And if we try to resist, if we don't go out and get a little action now and then, we're denying our biological imperative," Lynx concluded, and beamed, quite pleased with himself. He'd been working on his pitch for over three months, ever since he'd initially proposed going on a mission outside the Home and his cohorts had irately shot the idea down in verbal flames. But Lynx had refused to concede defeat. He'd been determined to go on a run no matter what it took.

Why should the other Warriors have all the fun?

There were 18 Warriors responsible for protecting the Home and safeguarding the Family. They were divided into fighting groups designated as Triads: Alpha, Beta, Gamma, Omega, Zulu, and Bravo. Lynx and his friends comprised Bravo. And while most of the other Warriors had been given the opportunity to venture far afield on dangerous assignments, Bravo Triad had not.

Lynx wanted to change that.

He had devised a devious scheme. The key to his strategy lay in persuading the top Warrior, Blade, to take them along. To that end he had gone to each of the other Warriors and ever so tactfully mentioned the fact Bravo Triad hadn't seen any real action in ages and that their skills were starting to deteriorate from the extended inactivity. When the other Warriors, natural fighters that they were, had commiserated and kindly expressed a wish that they could help, Lynx had coyly suggested they should make a mention of the fact to Blade and recommend Bravo Triad go on a run. Lynx had asked the other Warriors to refrain from mentioning his name when they talked to the giant.

And his ploy had worked!

Lynx almost snickered at the thought of his triumph. Instead, he kept a straight face and asked Ferret, "What do you think?"

"I think you're insane."

"You've got to admit my argument has merit."

"We've been all through this before, airhead. Gremlin and I don't want to go on a mission. Go by yourself and leave us alone."

"But we're a team," Lynx protested, alarmed by the realization his own buddies might ruin his carefully laid plans.

"Don't remind us," Ferret cracked.

Peeved, Lynx turned to Gremlin. "What do you say?"

"You already know, yes?"

"Isn't there anything I can do to make you guys change your minds?"

Ferret and Gremlin answered, loudly, in unison. "No!"

His shoulders sagging, Lynx walked a few yards to the north and sat down on a log. The perfect picture of depression, he rested his elbows on his knees and his chin in his palms. "Well, if that's your final decision, there's no sense in trying to persuade you. I know when I'm licked. And I'm not the type to try and take advantage of the best pals a guy could have.''

"Oh, brother," Ferret said.

Gremlin took a few steps toward the cat-man, sadness tinging his countenance. "We're sorry, yes? We didn't mean to hurt your feelings, no.''

"That's okay. I understand," Lynx replied, and vented a protracted sigh. "I don't blame you for being mad. Not at all. You were always level with me. You told me no months ago and I went and tried to pull a fast one on you. I'm scum. I know it.''

Gremlin took another pace. "You're not scum, no.''

"Yeah. I'm no better than horse manure," Lynx declared emotionally. "After all we've been through together, after we survived the war between the Federation and the Doktor, after we survived being captured by those android geeks down in Houston, after we laid our lives on the line for each other again and again, I pull a stunt like this." He shook his head. "I'm not worthy of your friendship.''

"You are, yes," Gremlin stated. He walked over and placed his right hand on the cat-man's shoulder. "Don't talk like this, no. It's not like you, yes?''

Lynx lifted a face reflecting profound sorrow. "Maybe I should ask to be transferred to another Triad.''

"Never!" Gremlin exclaimed, extremely upset by the proposal. "We're the Three Musketeers, yes? We always stick together, no? Through thick and thin.''

"Good old Gremlin," Lynx said, and patted the hand on his shoulder. "We can always count on you, can't we? You know, I've never told you this before, but I've always believed that out of all the hybrids the damn Doktor created, out of all us freaks in his menagerie, you were the kindest, the most noble.''

"Really?" Gremlin responded, genuinely moved by the compliment. "I had no idea, no.''

"Oh, brother," Ferret grumbled.

"Yep," Lynx went on. "Maybe that's why the bastard performed all those operations on your brain and made you talk the way you do. He couldn't stand havin' created something decent for once, so he made you the guinea pig in some of his stinkin' experiments."

"Gremlin always wondered why the Doktor singled him out, yes?" Gremlin mentioned.

"Now you know," Lynx said.

Gremlin stepped to one side and gazed at the blue sky. "Doktor was an evil, evil man, no?"

"The Doktor was slime," Lynx concurred. "And just think of how many more lives the bastard would have ruined if we hadn't wasted him."

"Blade did the wasting," Ferret interjected.

"Well, yeah, technically, I suppose," Lynx acknowledged reluctantly, then fell silent for all of ten seconds. "It's too bad, isn't it?"

"What is, yes?" Gremlin asked.

"That killin' that chump didn't do much to make this world a better place to live in. I mean, new threats are croppin' up all the time. Sometimes it seems like hardly a month goes by without someone or something tryin' to destroy the Home and wipe out the Family, who have to be the nicest bunch of people around."

"I remember you telling us once that the Family is so devoted to the Spirit, so involved with loving one another and being kind and courteous and all, that they make you want to puke," Ferret noted.

"I said that years ago, back when I didn't know any better," Lynx stated.

"You still don't know any better."

The cat-man ignored Ferret and looked at Gremlin again. "You see my point, don't you?"

"What point, yes?"

"About the real reason I wanted us to go on a run. It wasn't so much for me or us, but for the Family. Look at how nice they've been to us. They took us in after the Doktor died and allowed us to become full-fledged Family members. We eat three squares a day and have a roof over our heads when we want one. And they never ask for nothin' in return except that we pull our own weight as Warriors.''

"Very true, yes," Gremlin agreed.

Lynx stared dejectedly at the grass. "So what if I wanted to do the right thing and go on our fair share of the missions. So what if I think we owe the Family for all the kindness they've shown us. I shouldn't have volunteered our Triad without first consulting you two."

"You are a good hybrid, no?"

"Now I'm the one who feels like he needs to puke," Ferret declared.

"Go ahead. Make fun of me all you want to," Lynx said. "I deserve it."

"You're a terrible martyr," Ferret commented.

"Lynx does have a point, yes?" Gremlin pointed out, turning around.

"Yeah. On the top of his head," Ferret replied.

"Maybe we should do more to help the Family, no?"

"We're doing enough as it is."

"But Gremlin likes the Family. Gremlin wants to do more."

"Don't tell me you're falling for his bull?" Ferret asked.

"Lynx makes sense, yes?"

"Lynx hasn't made sense since day one. Can't you see he's trying to manipulate us again? He's scamming us, Gremlin."

The humanoid glanced at the cat-man. "Are you, yes?"

"Would I jive you guys?" Lynx replied with an earnest expression. "Oh, sure, I might kid you every now and then. But what are friends for?"

Gremlin nodded and stared at Ferret. "There. You see, yes?"

"Did you happen to notice he didn't answer your question?"

"Sure he did, yes?"

"I give up!" Ferret declared in disgust. He walked to a nearby boulder and took a seat. "If the two of you want to go off and slay dragons, be my guest. But I'm staying right here at the Home."

"What can one run hurt, yes?"

"It can get us killed," Ferret reiterated irritably.

Lynx came off the log in a rush and moved over to the boulder. "Not if we stick together and cover each other's backs like always. We're the best Triad in the Family and here's our chance to prove it."

"You two go prove it."

"Does this mean you'll let us go off by ourselves to get racked?"

Ferret glanced up. "That's a low blow, even for you."

"Don't be such a party-pooper. Come with us."

"No."

"Please, Ferret," Gremlin chimed in. "For me, yes? We should always stick together, no?"

A look of severe exasperation etched Ferret's face as he gazed from one to the other. They were as dear to him as life itself, his closest comrades, the brothers he'd never had. The mere notion of them being harmed was almost more than he could bear. Life without them would be empty and lonely. Under the circumstances, and even though he knew Lynx had outmaneuvered them again, his options were limited to just one. "All right," he catipulated wearily. "I'll go on the damn run to New Orleans."

Lynx impulsively embraced Ferret, then spun in a circle and whooped at the top of his lungs. "Look out, world! Here we come!"

"You did the right thing, yes," Gremlin assured Ferret.

"Did I? I hope so," Ferret said. He didn't bother to add that, soon, they could all be pushing up daisies.

CHAPTER
TWO

He stood on the western rampart, his hands clasped loosely behind his broad back, a veritable giant of a man attired in a black leather vest, green fatigue pants, and combat boots. Dark hair crowned his handsome head. His brooding gray eyes stared absently at the cleared field to the west of the 20-foot-high brick wall on which he was perched. Around his slim waist were strapped a pair of matching Bowies snug in their brown sheathes. His bulging muscles radiated an aura of sheer power even when at rest. To a casual observer he might have appeared to be a statue, a bronzed superman sculpted by an artist who intended to invest the piece with the strength of a Hercules. Not one of those mighty sinews so much as quivered as the giant contemplated the personal problem he faced, a dilemma that could be summed up succinctly in two words.

Not again!

His impending departure for New Orleans in the morning had aggravated a raw emotional wound, had angered his wife, Jenny, and caused yet another spat related to his prolonged absences from the Home.

Not that he could blame her. Or his son, Gabe, who had been upset to learn they wouldn't be going fishing tomorrow as he had promised. If only they could appreciate his position!

What other choice did he have?

He was, after all, the head Warrior. The safety of over a hundred lives and the guardianship of the 30-acre compound in which they all lived were ultimately his responsibility. And he would protect both with his dying breath, if need be.

The Home and the Family. Both had come into existence shortly before the outbreak of World War Three, which had occurred 106 years ago. The Founder of the Home and the family, a wealthy, idealistic filmmaker named Kurt Carpenter, had wisely foreseen the impending Armageddon and taken steps to ensure his ideals survived his lifetime. Carpenter had expended a fortune to have the Home constructed, then instituted a social system designed to ensure individual liberty while maximizing human potential.

The Founder had realized the necessity for a security unit and created the Warrior class, just as other group needs were met by the formation of other appropriate classes: the Tillers, the Weavers, the Healers, the Elders, and others. Each performed an important function, and none were considered superior to any others. Carpenter had despised inequality and hypocrisy in any form, and he had taken concrete steps to promote freedom for all while hopefully eliminating the rise of the vulture class, those who enjoyed lording it over their peers, those the Family dubbed vile power-mongers.

Only one power-monger had arisen within the Family in its entire history, but the same could not be said of the outside world, where demented dictators and repressive city-states had arisen to fill the vacuum left by the collapse of the United States government.

The giant frowned, thinking of all the enemies the Family had faced, all the foes who would gladly destroy the Home without so much as a second thought. There were the Technics, the Superiors, the Soviets, the Dragons, the Gild, the Peers, and many more. If not for the Warriors, the Family would have long since been eliminated. And one of the keys to the Warriors' success lay in their resolve to meet any and all threats head-on, to venture wherever necessary to terminate menaces as the danger arose.

Why let the enemy come to them when they could take the fight to the enemy?

The question prompted a sigh from the top Warrior. As if his post at the Home wasn't enough of a reason for his constant absences, he also served as the leader of the Freedom Force, the elite strike team consisting of a volunteer from each of the seven factions comprising the Freedom Federation. The Family had found allies as well as enemies far beyond the brick walls, and six of those friendly factions had joined with the descendants of Carpenter's followers to form the Federation.

So was it any wonder he spent so much time away from his loved ones?

If the safety of the Home and Family was imperiled, he had to deal with the threat. If any Federation faction was attacked or came up against a danger they couldn't handle, he had to handle it. His responsibilities, sometimes, intimidated even him. But he wouldn't shirk them as long as breath remained in his body. He had pledged to perform his duties faithfully, and a man could be measured by the value of his word.

Just two days ago he had arrived at the Home after spending a week in Los Angeles, where the Force was based, planning to spend the next 14 days with Jenny and Gabe and attending to routine business at the Home. How was he to know that only last night the man assigned to monitor the shortwave radio they had confiscated from the Russians would receive a distress call from, of all places, New Orleans? Ever since one of the other Warriors, his close friend Hickok, had picked up an SOS from Seattle almost two years ago, the Family had regularly monitored the shortwave band for emergency signals.

Last night they'd hit pay dirt.

Which figured!

If perfect timing were gold, he'd be a pauper. Everything seemed to happen to him at the worst possible moment. He often suspected that the infamous Murphy hovered over his head simply waiting for the ideal opportunity to zap him.

Such as now.

Jenny and Gabe might not have objected so strenuously if the distress call had been received in another week or two—after they had had time to be together and savor the experience of being a family again. But coming so soon after his return to the compound from the Free State of California, the emergency request had thrown a monumental monkey wrench into his home life.

So what else was new?

Finally he moved, raising his arms to stretch as he inhaled the cool October air. His eyes strayed to the aircraft parked in the middle of the field beyond. The Hurricane, a jet endowed with vertical-takeoff-or-landing capability, was one of two such craft possessed by the California military. The VTOLs were the lifeblood of the Federation. They were utilized as a monthly courier service, carrying messages from one Federation faction to another. They transported Federation heads to summit meetings. They carried the Force on assignments. And, as with the one in the field, they conveyed the giant to and from the Home on a regular basis. Two days ago the Hurricane before him had brought him from L.A. The pilot had decided to stay over an extra day to conduct minor maintenance, and it was well he did. Because now the giant intended to have the VTOL fly him to New Orleans so he could investigate the call they had received.

Along with the three hybrids.

He saw someone step into view from behind the Hurricane, the Warrior guarding the aircraft, and he smiled and waved.

The sentry, a wiry man wearing forest-green clothing that contrasted with his blond hair and jutting blond beard, carried a compound bow. Strapped to his back was a large quiver of arrows. "Yo, Blade!" he called out, and waved back.

"Teucer!" Blade replied, lowering his arm.

The bowman continued in a slow circuit of the jet, alertly scanning the treeline farther to the west.

A good man, Blade thought to himself, and placed his hands on the hilts of his Bowies. All of the Warriors were good men or women or—

"What the dickens are you doing up here all by your lonesome, pard?"

The familiar voice brought a grin to the giant's face, and he pivoted to see his two fellow members of Alpha Triad ascending the wooden stairs to the rampart.

In the lead, wearing buckskins, came another blond man, only this one was leaner than Teucer and sported a mustache but no beard. In a holster on either hip rode a Colt Python revolver. He had his thumbs hooked in his gunbelt and a typical nonchalant smile creasing his countenance. When he spoke again, he did so in his customary Old West fashion. "Are you expectin' a passel of mangy owlhoots to attack the Home?"

"Not hardly, Hickok," Blade replied.

The gunfighter stepped onto the rampart and strolled casually over to the giant. "We stopped by your homestead and your missus told us you'd moseyed this way."

"One of these days this dummy will speak normal English and put the rest of us in total shock," commented the second man, a stocky Indian who favored green clothing and who had tucked a genuine tomahawk under his brown leather belt. Both his eyes and his hair were dark. His heritage was Blackfoot.

"Don't you know it," Blade agreed, chuckling.

Hickok glanced at their Indian companion. "Hardy-har-har. Who died and made you a language expert, Geronimo?"

"It doesn't take an expert to know you're ninety-nine bricks shy of a hundred-brick load."

"I didn't know you could count that high without takin' off your socks and shoes," Hickok quipped.

Geronimo stopped and stared idly at the Hurricane. "At least it doesn't take me ten minutes to tie my moccasin laces in the morning."

Blade, who knew their banter could continue for hours if not checked, decided to interrupt the two best friends he'd had since childhood. "To what do I owe this dubious honor?"

"Dubious?" Hickok repeated. "Our comin' up here to palaver had nothin' to do with makin' knights."

Blade had to think about that one for a few seconds before he understood. He grimaced and scrutinized both men. "Then why are you up here?"

"Do you want to tell him or should I?" Hickok asked Geronimo.

"Be my guest."

"Fine," the gunman said. He faced the giant squarely and adopted a slightly miffed expression. "What's this we hear about you not takin' us to New Orleans?"

"You heard correctly," Blade answered.

"But we're a Triad, dag nab it! We're supposed to work as a team. We've been on more runs together than any of the other Warriors."

"Which is precisely the reason I want to take others with me," Blade mentioned. "You know we have to give the rest of the Warriors a chance to see the outside world while honing their combat skills."

"Maybe so," Hickok acknowledged, "but you seem to be going a mite overboard with this business. You didn't take us to Boston, you didn't take us to Green Bay, and now you're waltzin' off to New Orleans without us."

"Boston?" Blade said. "You can't be serious. I was kidnapped and taken there against my will. How can you blame me for that?"

The gunfighter pursed his lips. "Okay. Maybe you had a legitimate excuse. But what about Green Bay?"

"The Technics were involved. I hoped to give Yama a chance to come to grips with his hatred for them."

"If you ask me, pard, Yama hates those coyotes even

more," Hickok noted.

"I agree," Geronimo chimed in. "The other day he asked me if I believed a single man could assault Technic City and survive."

Blade tensed. "He what?"

"That's right," Geronimo confirmed. "I told him the idea was crazy."

"How did he react?"

"Yama gave me this funny sort of smile," Geronimo disclosed.

"Uh-oh," Hickok said.

Blade shifted and surveyed the compound, searching for a sign of the Warrior in blue, the man universally regarded as the living equal of the Hindu King of Death from whom Yama had taken his name. As with every other Family member, Yama had gone through a special Naming ceremony on the occasion of his sixteenth birthday and selected the unusual appellation for his very own. There was no sign of the gray-haired Warrior anywhere near the west wall. "I'll have to have a long talk with him after I get back."

"Do you want us to keep our peepers on him while you're gone?" Hickok offered.

"Yes," Blade said. "Make certain he doesn't do anything foolish."

"We'll try our best," Geronimo stated. "But if that guy decides to leave without authorization, it'll take more than the two of us to stop him."

"Bull," Hickok declared. "It'll be a piece of cake."

"How do you figure?" Geronimo rejoined. "Yama is almost as big and strong as Blade. He's as competent a martial artist as Rikki-Tikki-Tavi. He can shoot a revolver nearly as expertly as you. In fact, he's an expert with *every* weapon in our armory, unlike the rest of us, who have specialized in only one or two. How will you stop him?"

"Easy." Hickok snickered. "We'll use my secret weapon."

"Your breath?"

"No, rocks-for-brains. I happen to have heard from a reliable source that Yama has a weakness no one knows about."

"Who's your source?"

"Yama's niece," Hickok revealed.

Geronimo glanced at Blade, who shrugged to indicate he had no idea what the gunman was talking about, then back at Hickok. "What could Marian possibly know that the rest of us don't?"

The gunfighter made a show of scanning their immediate vicinity, verifying no one was eavesdropping. Then he leaned forward and whispered conspiratorially. "Yama is ticklish."

A look of utter astonishment froze Geronimo's features.

"See? I knew you'd be impressed," Hickok gloated.

"Only by your stupidity."

"Did you know he's ticklish?"

"That's not the point, mush-mind."

"Then what is?" Hickok asked.

Geronimo rolled his eyes skyward, then became serious. "Let me put it to you this way. Do you *really* expect to best Yama by tickling him?"

"Yep. I've got it all figured out. Rikki, Samson, Spartacus, Ares, Sundance, and you will hold him down while I tickle him until he surrenders."

"Wait a minute. Why do you get to do the tickling while the rest of us are in danger of having every bone in our body broken?"

"Because it's *my* plan."

"Has it ever occurred to you that the only reason Yama is ticklish when he's with his niece is because he relaxes enough in her presence to let down his guard? Has it occurred to you that Yama is well known for his self-control, and if we try to tickle him there's the dinstinct likelihood he won't *want* to be tickled?"

"That's where Plan B comes in handy."

"Plan B?"

"Yep. If the tickling doesn't work, then Teucer, Shane, and Achilles will tie Yama up while the rest of you pin him down."

"And what will you be doing while all this is going on?"

"Supervising."

"I see. The rest of us put our lives on the line, and you goof off as usual."

"I don't goof off. Plannin' is hard work. And remember, when Blade is gone *I'm* in charge. I'm the brains of the outfit," Hickok said, and surreptitiously winked at the giant.

"How can you be the brains when everyone knows you've had a lobotomy?" Geronimo asked.

"Oh, yeah? And just why do you reckon the Big Guy picked me to be the head honcho while he's away?"

"Obviously not for your good looks."

"Exactly. Hey, wait a minute!"

"So it must have been because Blade has a terrific sense of humor," Geronimo said. He looked at the man in question. "Am I right?"

Blade smiled and shook his head slowly. "Already I'm looking forward to the peace and quiet of this mission."

"Who are you takin' anyway?" Hickok inquired.

"Bravo Triad."

"Bravo," Hickok said, his eyes widening slightly. "You're takin' the furballs and Gremlin instead of us?"

"Yep."

"I'm surprised. I thought you were aimin' to hold off takin' them along for a spell?"

"I was going to hold off, but a number of other Warriors have approached me to request that I take Lynx on a run just so he'll stop pestering them," Blade related, then chuckled. "Actually, they've *begged* me to take him along."

"Do you figure Tabby will behave himself for once?" Hickok remarked.

"I hope so," Blade said. "If he doesn't, only Gremlin, Ferret, and I will be coming back."

The gunman laughed. "Don't get our hopes up!"

Geronimo folded his arms and stared intently at the head Warrior. "So what was this message Seth Mason received?"

"Seth picked up a distress call originating from New Orleans—or near the city, evidently. We have the map coordinates and the Hurricane should be able to drop us right at the spot," Blade said. "The signal wasn't very strong and Seth had trouble tuning it in. When he tried to contact the sender to get a clarification, he was unable to reach the other party. Either their set is malfunctioning or they were operating on weak batteries. In any event, Seth received enough to indicate the people in New Orleans are in dire straits."

"How so?" Geronimo queried.

"The radio operator in New Orleans claimed the people are struggling to overthrow the Black Snake Society."

"The what?" Hickok interjected.

"That's all Seth knows. The message kept breaking up and several of the words were garbled or unintelligible. An organization called the Black Snake Society has control of New Orleans and the people there want help in achieving their freedom."

"Doesn't sound like a lot to go on," Geronimo mentioned with a touch of concern.

"It's not," Blade admitted. "The transmission was cut off in mid-sentence. Seth stayed on the frequency for an hour but the caller never came back on. We were lucky Seth stumbled on the call in the first place. He told me that he had received part of the same or a similar transmission five days before. There were only a few sentences, and not enough information for him to ascertain the point of origination."

"What if it's a trap, pard?" Hickok asked.

"I doubt it."

"I seem to recollect a certain mutation by the name of Manta usin' a phony distress call to lure in slaves for his kelp factory in Seattle," Hickok mentioned. "How do you know this isn't another phony?''

Blade gazed to the west. ''I don't, but there's only one way to discover the truth.''

''How much time are you alloting yourself for the mission?'' Geronimo questioned.

''One week. Captain Laslo will drop us off tomorrow afternoon. He's under orders to return to the site in seven days and retrieve us. If we're not there, he'll fly directly to the Home and inform you.''

''In which case we'll fly back down there and tear the city apart,'' Hickok proposed.

''You'll do no such thing.''

''Bet me.''

''I'm serious, Nathan. Sending Warriors down there to try and find us would needlessly endanger their lives.''

''Needlessly? A Warrior never abandons another Warrior. Never. If you're not at the rendezvous site, I'll personally fly down there and perforate noggins until I find you.''

''For once he's right,'' Geronimo added. ''You can't honestly expect us to do nothing.''

''I order you not to attempt a rescue.''

Hickok suddenly started swatting the side of his head, slapping his palm on his right ear. ''If this ain't the darnedest thing. My blamed ears just went on the fritz. I can't hear a word you say.''

''You can't, huh?''

''Nope.''

''Then how come you just answered me?''

''Would you believe I read your lips?''

Blade glanced at both of them. ''I mean it. If you guys disobey me, there'll be hell to pay.'' He walked to the stairs and headed down.

The gunfighter waited until the giant was halfway to the bottom before he leaned toward Geronimo. ''Now what do you reckon that was all about?''

''I wish I knew.''

''He can't be serious.''

"He *sounds* serious."

Hickok straightened and moved to the first step. "Well, if you ask me he's been standin' in the sun too long."

"We will go after him if he doesn't return?"

"Do bears crap in the woods?"

"I've heard a rumor to that effect."

The gunman snapped his fingers and smiled. "Hey, I've got me a great idea."

"Uh-oh."

"If the Big Guy doesn't come back on schedule, we'll take Yama with us to New Orleans. He's in the mood to kick tail, and those goons down there won't last two seconds."

"How do you know?" Geronimo inquired.

"Give me a break, pard. How tough can they be with a corny name like the Black Snake Society? I'll bet they're a bunch of wimps."

"I hope you're right."

CHAPTER THREE

Louisiana. The 18th state to enter the Union, the 33rd largest in the United States. One of the few to have more than one nickname. Known as the Creole State because of the many Creoles who lived there, descendants of the early Spanish and French settlers. Also known as the Pelican State, due to the thousands of brown pelicans inhabiting the marshes along the coast, and the Sugar Cane State, based on the huge quantities of sugar cane Louisiana produced each year prior to the war.

More importantly, when the missiles were launched, Louisiana had a population of approximately five million and about 300 incorporated cities, towns, and villages. Seventy percent of the population had lived in the rural areas. In addition to the Creoles, a large number of Cajuns had also lived in the state. They were descendants of Acadians from Canada.

Three land regions dominated the former state: the West Gulf Coastal Plain, the Mississippi Alluvial Plain, and the East Gulf Coastal Plain in which New Orleans was located. Flooding had been a constant problem for those living in the

lower areas. Tons of silt carried by the rivers had raised the
level of the riverbeds above the surrounding countryside, and
several major floods had reportedly covered a third of the
state.

The climate was hot, humid, and subtropical. Louisiana
had been rated as one of the wettest states with an annual
rainfull of 56 inches, although the southern section had
recorded receiving over a hundred inches of rain periodically.

All of these facts Blade reviewed as he hiked along a game
trail and wiped his right forearms across his perspiring brow.
He'd spent an hour in the Family library researching the state
the night before. In his back left pocket was a map. He
squinted up at the bright afternoon sun, marveling at the
drastic change in weather between extreme northwestern
Minnesota, where the Home was located, and extreme
southern Louisiana. A mild cold front had lowered
temperatures at the Home overnight, but here, thanks to the
subtropical climate, the temperature hovered in the eighties
and the humid air seemed to drip moisture.

From the air, as the Hurricane swept in from the northwest,
Blade had noted an interesting fact. Apparently another major
flood had occurred, and the city of New Orleans was almost
completely ringed by swampy bayous, cut off from the inland
regions by a formidable expanse of inhospitable marsh
infested by alligators, snakes, and swarms of insects. He
hoped they could avoid going into the swamps.

"Damn, it's hot!"

Blade glanced over his right shoulder at the three hybrids
following him, each attired in the usual loincloth, and
grinned. Over their strenuous objections, he had compelled
them to bring a weapon along. All three had opted for an
AR-15. They also carried spare magazines in pouches
strapped around their waists. "Quit your griping, Lynx,"
he said.

"You didn't tell me this place would fry my fur," the cat-
man groused.

"No one twisted your arm to make you come along,"

Blade noted, adjusting the backpack he wore. "You're here of your own free will." ·

"I wish I could say the same," Ferret muttered.

Blade glanced at the second mutation. "What do you mean? Lynx told me all three of you were eager to go on a mission. He said you'd appointed him as your spokesman to present your appeal."

"He did, did he?" Ferret said, glaring at his feline companion.

A snicker came from Gremlin, who brought up the rear. "Where would we be without kind, considerate Lynx to look out for us, yes?"

"Did he lie to me?" Blade asked bluntly, halting.

The hybrids stopped. Lynx cast an apprehensive gaze at his friends.

"I won't tolerate a Warrior who lies," Blade declared. "He assured me that both of you wanted to come along. Is that true?"

For a second no one spoke.

Ferret sighed and stared off into the distance. "Yeah, it's true. We couldn't wait to go on a run with you."

Blade looked at Gremlin. "Is that right?"

The humanoid simply nodded.

"Okay, then. I don't want any griping from any of you. Whatever happens, you asked to be here," Blade reminded them, and continued tramping eastward. He suspected Ferret and Gremlin were covering for their buddy, but he wouldn't press the issue. Actually, he was pleased at the loyalty they exhibited to one another. Triad members were supposed to be supremely committed companions.

Lynx, eager to change the topic, voiced a question. "Why are we out here in the middle of nowhere, miles from the city?"

"Because these are the coordinates where the distress call originated," Blade said.

"You must have the wrong coordinates. There's nothin' here but bugs and birds."

Blade surveyed the land around them. Cypress, oak, and pine trees grew in abundance. Varieties of birds he had never seen before winged overhead or roosted in the trees. The soil underfoot felt soft, almost spongy. Before the Hurricane had landed in a large clearing to the west, as it flew in at treetop level to avoid being spotted from afar, he'd observed bayous to the north, south, and west. There might be more swampland to the east, which meant they were on an elevated tract of dry land. He'd also observed a wide field or meadow on the east side, and had selected it as their immediate goal.

"I smell something," Lynx declared, tilting his head to sniff the air loudly.

"Human scent?" Blade asked, looking back.

"Nope. Just a rabbit."

"I smell it too," Ferret mentioned.

"Yeah, but I detected the scent first," Lynx bragged.

Blade faced forward and pushed a limb aside that blocked the trail. "What difference does it make?"

"It makes a big different to Lynx," Ferret explained. "He's always trying to prove his senses are sharper than ours."

"They are," Lynx declared.

"Your hearing is keener than that of most humans, isn't it?" Blade asked, although he already knew the answer.

"You know it," Lynx stated proudly. "So is my eyesight, my sense of smell, and my reflexes. Compared to me most humans are pathetic."

"I'm lucky I brought you along then," Blade said, his tone only marginally sarcastic. "And since your ears function so well, you should have no difficulty understanding me when I tell you that we should consider ourselves in enemy territory and only talk when absolutely essential. Understood?"

"Why are you pickin' on me? The others were yakkin' too."

"You broke silence first."

"Excuse me for living."

Blade grinned, moving to the right as the trail curved,

skirting a dense thicket. In 20 yards the path led due east again and he increased speed, anxious to reach the field, to find the party responsible for sending the distress call. He reasoned there must be a habitation of some sort nearby, a place where the radio could be sheltered from the elements. Unless, of course, someone had traveled all the way out to this spot at night just to make the broadcasts, which wouldn't be very practical.

The cardinal flew over the path from right to left.

The Warrior's eyes narrowed at the sight of an open tract ahead. Rather abruptly the trees thinned and in front of them stretched the field. Not 40 yards from the treeline stood a neglected wooden cabin. The walls were in desperate need of a paint job and the roof sagged in the center, threatening to collapse with the next heavy rain. A sole window in the middle of the wall resembled a blank, lifeless eye.

No activity could be perceived inside.

Blade stepped behind an oak tree and watched the cabin for several minutes, waiting to learn if anyone was home. But nothing happened. He looked at the hybrids, who were likewise concealed in the shelter of nearby tree trunks, and issued instructions. "We'll go in fast. Single file. Stay low and keep close to me."

"Wouldn't it be better if we fanned out?" Lynx responded.

"When I want you to fan out, I'll let you know," Blade said brusquely. "Let's go." He clutched the submachine gun he'd elected to bring along on the mission, a Thompson M1A1, hunched over, and ran toward the cabin. His favorite SMG, a Commando Arms Carbine, was being overhauled by the Family Gunsmiths, and he'd opted for the Thompson because the two were very similiar and he was accustomed to the feel and performance of the Commando.

No one challenged them as they raced forward.

Blade reached the side of the building first and crouched down, listening. Once the others were to his left he eased to the corner and peeked around the edge.

Not a soul was in sight.

"Stay close," the Warrior reiterated in a whisper, and
darted from cover to sprint to the front of the cabin. He
paused again at the corner to scan the field and the front of
the structure, bothered at finding the door wide open. Surely
whoever sent the message wouldn't go off and leave the cabin
unattended? He inched along the wall to within a foot of the
doorway, then stopped.

The waist-high weeds in the field were stirred slightly by
a sluggish breeze from the northwest. Bees, a few butter-
flies, and other insects were in evidence, but nothing else.

"I don't like this, Boss," Lynx whispered, sliding up
beside the giant.

"Don't talk," Blade hissed, and swung into the doorway,
his knees bent, sweeping the Thompson from side to side.

The cabin was unoccupied. A rickety wooden table sat off
to the right, and a chair had been positioned on either side.
Those three items were the only furniture.

Blade stepped inside, checked behind the door even though
it hung almost flush with the wall, and walked over to the table.
He thoughtfully gnawed on his lower lip, pondering the
implications. His first assumption was that no one had used
the cabin in ages, that perhaps he did have the wrong
coordinates. Then he glanced at the windowsills and the floor
and realized someone had been there, and quite recently. Dust
caked all the sills and the floor space nearest the walls, but
the table, the chairs, and most of the floor were all dust free.
So perhaps the cabin had been the site from which the
broadcasts had originated.

But where was the broadcaster?

The Warrior returned to the doorway and stood gazing at
the countryside to the east. A very faint trail was visible
leading in that direction.

"Can I speak, oh, mighty one?" Lynx inquired.

"What is it?"

"If you ask me, this is turnin' into a waste of our time."

"No one asked you."

"What do we do now? Sit around and twiddle our thumbs

until someone shows up?''

"We might," Blade said. He stepped outside and moved a dozen yards from the structure, debating their course of action. Perhaps whoever had made the calls only did so at night. In that case, the person with the radio might not put in an appearance until nightfall. They could scour every nook and cranny, or they could stay there and hope someone came.

Ferret walked a few paces to the north, his nostrils quivering. "Do you smell that?" he asked, glancing at Lynx.

"What?"

"I'm not exactly sure. A reptilian sort of scent, one I've never encountered before."

"Yeah. I smelled it a while back. Beats me what it could be," the cat-man stated.

"Snakes, maybe?" Blade suggested.

"I know snake scent," Lynx said. "It's faint and very distinct. This is a stronger odor, and different."

"Alligators, then," Blade remarked.

"Or an unknown kind of mutation, yes?" Gremlin interjected.

"Whatever it is, it gives me the willies," Ferret mentioned.

Bladde raised his right hand to shield his eyes from the sunlight. Far off on the eastern horizon towering buildings were barely visible. Skyscrapers, most likely. Downtown New Orleans. He estimated the distance at four or five miles.

"What's the plan, Fearless Leader?" Lynx queried. "Your wish is our command."

"Tell you what," Blade said. "Since you're so antsy to do something, why don't you take that trail over there and see where it leads?" He pointed eastward.

"My pleasure," the cat-man replied promptly, and took off. "Don't wait up for me, Mother!" He jogged into the field.

"Be back here in thirty minutes!" Blade ordered.

Lynx looked over his left shoulder and smirked. "I don't own a watch." With that he cackled and broke into a trot, only his chest, slim shoulders, and head in view above the tops of the swaying vegatation.

"Lynx is a card, no?" Gremlin commented.

"No," Ferret responded.

"I can think of other words that would fit him better," Blade said. He walked back to the cabin and sat down in the doorway, leaning his back against the right-hand jamb.

"Lynx means well, yes."

"Is that why he persuaded you to come along on this assignment against your better judgment?" Blade asked.

Ferret and Gremlin exchanged startled looks.

"You knew all the time, no?" the humanoid said.

"I do now," Blade said.

"Don't be hard on Lynx," Ferret stated. "He can't help himself. The damn Doktor bred all of us to be exactly as we are. I'm a moody cuss, Gremlin is always Mr. Cheerful, and Lynx just naturally believes he's right all of the time. Unfortunately for his ego and the rest of us, he's correct about eighty-five percent of the time. And if you ever tell him I said so, I'll deny every word."

Blade smiled and rested the Thompson in his lap. He debated whether to open the backpack and remove a few strips of jerked venison, but before he could reach a decision a series of sharp retorts from the direction Lynx had taken brought him to his feet.

Gunshots!

CHAPTER
FOUR

Lynx chuckled as he jogged eastward. So far the mission had been on the dull side, although he had been able to alleviate the monotony by baiting Blade. His conscience nagged at him about taunting the giant so much, but he simply couldn't help himself. Contrariness was an integral part of his feline nature, as much a part of him as his fur or his razor-sharp nails. Besides, Blade invited such treatment by his somber attitude and strict devotion to proper procedure. The giant was a perfectionist, and perfectionists just naturally got Lynx's goat.

A garter snake slithered across the path four feet in front of him.

Abruptly slowing, Lynx warily watched the reptile even though it was harmless. He disliked snakes intensely. They gave him the creeps. And he invariably went out of his way to avoid them where possible. He chided himself for not realizing there would be a lot of snakes in Louisiana.

The tip of the garter snake's thin tail disappeared in the weeds.

Good riddance, sucker! Lynx thought, and forced onward.

The presence of the snake prompted him to think of other unsavory creatures, like alligators and spiders. He'd never encountered a gator before, but spiders ranked high up there with snakes as creatures the planet could better do without.

The scent of deer wafted to his sensitive nostrils.

Lynx almost turned aside to stalk the animals. He was starting to become hungry, and fresh venison would taste delicious. Just thinking about a mouthful of raw, bloody meat made him salivate. He'd have to talk to the Big Dummy about allowing them to do some hunting after he returned to the cabin. Neither he nor his friends had brought backpacks; they'd opted to travel light and fast, to live off the land as befitted their bestial natures.

Even Gremlin.

Which was odd.

Lynx wondered why Gremlin tried so hard to emulate Ferret and him. Of the three of them, Gremlin possessed the least animalistic nature. While Ferret and Lynx were half-man, half-beast, Gremlin was essentially a strange-looking human. A human endowed with exceptional strength and stamina, true, but nonetheless more like Homo sapiens than Lynx or Ferret could ever hope to be.

Sometimes Lynx found himself envying Gremlin, but only in extremely rare moments of emotional weakness when he pondered the stigma attached to his own state of being. Most humans regarded hybrids with either disdain, mistrust, or outright hatred for no other reason than the fact that hybrids were different. And Lynx had never been able to tolerate such a repugnant attitude. It wasn't *his* fault he was a damned mutation. The rotten Doktor deserved the dubious credit for his condition.

Ahhhh, yes.

The Doktor.

Lynx smiled at the memory of how the Doktor had looked after Blade got through with the scumbag. He only wished he could have done the job himself. He'd tried to assassinate the Doktor once and wound up in a cage, slated for extermination. If not for a Warrior named Yama, who had infiltrated the Doktor's Citadel in Cheyenne, Wyoming, where Lynx was being held, he wouldn't be alive today. Yama had turned out to be one tough mother, and together they had set the Doktor's plans back decades.

Those were the good old days.

Now he was lucky if he saw action once a month, and even then the "action" usually consisted of dealing with a wild animal or a rampaging mutation, such as a bear with two heads or a wolf with six legs. Deformed animals were quite common due to the massive amounts of radiation that had saturated the environment during and after World War Three.

Engrossed in reflection, Lynx advanced another 25 yards. To his left, perhaps 50 feet distant, stood a small stand of trees, not more than half a dozen, and he wouldn't have paid them more than fleeting attention if not for an unexpected bright gleam from among the trunks, the glinting of a metallic object in the brilliant sunlight.

Lynx reacted instinctively by vaulting forward with his arms extended, and he was in midair when the crack of automatic gunfire rent the humid atmosphere. He came down hard and heard the rounds zipping through the weeds all around him.

A trap!

They'd walked into a stinking trap!

Lynx rose into a crouch, staying below the top of the vegetation, and turned, intending to speed back to the others. His keen eyes registered movement in the weeds 15 yards to his rear, and he realized hidden foes had lain concealed while he passed them by. The wind would not have carried their scent if they were lying flush with the ground in the dense growth.

He'd been outfoxed.

Angered at his failure to detect the attackers, and frustrated because he couldn't retrace his route with an unknown number of enemies blocking his path, Lynx pivoted and dashed eastward, staying bent in half. His small stature

worked to his advantage. He could move at two thirds of
his top speed easily without having to worry about being seen.

After 30 feet he drew up short and gazed along his back
trail. Vague, black forms were in hot pursuit. They were
sticking to the weeds so he couldn't see them clearly. Just
for sheer spite, Lynx pointed his AR-15 at one of the
indistinct forms and squeezed the trigger.

The target screamed and pitched into the weeds.

Score one for our side! Lynx thought, and slipped into the
vegetation on his right. If he couldn't return to the cabin using
the path, he'd circle around the SOBs and rejoin his
companions.

A burst of automatic fire erupted from the vicinity of the
cabin.

Alarmed, Lynx angled to the west. The volume of noise
sounded as if World War Four was being conducted. What
if Ferret or Gremlin were killed? The horrifying prospect
galvanized him to increase his speed. He sped at a reckless
pace, heedless of the risk, parting the weeds with the barrel
of the AR-15, and moments later blundered into one of their
foes.

A squat figure materialized directly in front of him, a figure
who had been facing in the opposite direction but was
beginning to turn at the sound of Lynx's approach. A large
black man dressed in some sort of black uniform and wearing
mirrored sunglasses, he tried to bring a compact submachine
gun into play.

Lynx had scant time to be surprised at the unexpected
meeting. One second weeds were before him, the next the
man in black was raising his weapon not inches from the
tip of the AR-15. Lynx did the only thing he could do under
the circumstances. He fired at point-blank range.

The big black man took the slugs in the forehead and was
hurled backwards.

Other black shapes appeared, scattered in the weeds at
varying distances, and they cut loose at the hybrid.

Lynx threw himself rearward, then scrambled on his

elbows and knees to the south. There were more of them than he initially assumed, and he had to swing farther around to bypass them.

"Which way did he go?" someone shouted to the north.

"Why don't you tell the freak where you're at, you idiot!" another man replied, then added what sounded like curses in an unknown tongue.

What language was that? Lynx wondered. French, maybe. But he couldn't be certain. He'd only listened to French spoken once by a linguist at the Home who specialized in learning every frigging language on the planet. The language that guy had used might as well be Martian as far as he was concerned. At least he had a general idea of their position thanks to the lame-brain with the big mouth.

And there was one more good thing.

The firing had stopped.

Then again, Lynx thought, crawling rapidly, the silence could be a bad sign. It could mean Blade and his buddies were dead. If so, somebody would pay.

Oh, *how* they'd pay!

A voice louder than all the rest roared out a few words in the alien tongue, and suddenly the weeds were shrouded in total quiet.

Spooky. Real spooky.

Lynx shook his head to dispel the sensation of unease that gripped him. He was up against humans, and humans were hardly a threat to worry about. They were no match for his hypersenses; they couldn't hope to rival his speed or his steely sinews. Well, Blade could, but he didn't count because they were on the same side. And so could Yama, and Rikki-Tikki-Tavi, and—

Something crunched to the west.

Lynx halted, and castigated himself for allowing his mind to drift from the critical matter at hand. Who the hell cared whether a few of the Warriors were his equal? Now was not the time for pondering such nonsense.

Not if he wanted to live.

He rose up on his knees and peered intently through the green mat of slender strands, flowers, and bushes. At the limits of his vision someone or something moved, bearing to the north and away from him.

Good riddance, sucker!

Lynx pressed onward, keeping low, losing all track of time, although he guessed that 15 minutes elapsed before he halted, then swung to the west once more. Surely the men in black were all well north of his position?

Who were they anyway?

And what was with the black uniforms?

Lynx traversed 20 yards and unexpectedly came to a clearing. At least he believed the narrow track of open ground was a clearing until he brushed aside the last of the weeds and discovered he had emerged on the shallow bank of a body of stagnant water. He glanced to the south and found a bayou stretching for as far as the eye could see. A projecting arm of the marsh extended into the field. All he had to do was go around it.

A splash ruffled the placid surface of the water.

Startled, Lynx glanced down, studying the dark water, noting a few tiny fish swimming near the shore, where the pool was marginally clear, and an abundance of water lilies covering the top, concealing anything that might be lurking below. Farther out were high weeds.

There could be snakes down there.

Poisonous snakes.

Scowling distastefully at the likelihood, Lynx moved to the north.

A loud rustling occurred in the brush to the northwest, coming closer.

One of the men in black was heading straight for him!

Lynx grinned and slipped into the weeds. He crept to the north and paused near the point where the water ended. Instead of killing this one, he planned to take the man prisoner. Perhaps he could make the turkey talk. Any facts he could glean would improve his chances.

The noise was surprisingly loud. Either whoever approached entertained no qualms about his lack of stealth, or the person must be a first-rate klutz. Or an amateur, which essentially amounted to the same thing.

A figure appeared, only this one wore blue garments, not black.

Lynx tried to distinguish the person's features, but the compact vegetation prevented him. He deduced the amateur would pass within a yard of his position, and he eased slightly lower and released the AR-15.

Keep coming, dirtbag!

As if eager to oblige, the person advanced swiftly. Once a head of long, black hair was revealed for an instant, and then the weeds concealed the newcomer again.

Lynx beamed in anticipation. His steely sinews coiled, and when the person in blue was three feet away he suddenly rose up and pounced, leaping onto the human and bearing the amateur to the ground. They rolled several times, the person struggling furiously, and they wound up with Lynx astride his captive's chest, his knees pinning the captive's arms, his fingers formed into claws. He took one look and his eyes widened in amazement. "You're a woman!"

She was young and, as humans went, attractive, her own green eyes reflecting her shock. Her mouth hung wide and she scarcely breathed.

Bewildered, Lynx gazed all around them. There wasn't anyone nearby. He stared at his prisoner again and realized she did not have a weapon. "Who are you? What are you doing here?" he asked in a whisper.

Her lips moved but produced no words.

"I won't hurt you," Lynx assured her.

The woman abruptly opened her mouth as if to scream.

"No!" Lynx hissed, and clasped his right hand over her lips. "Not a peep out of you, sister. There are guys in black close by who are tryin' to waste me. If you make a sound, I'll rip your throat apart." He paused to give his words time to sink in. "If you understand, nod once."

She nodded.

"Good. I'm going to lift my hand, but if you try any tricks the same thing applies. Nod if you promise to keep your yap shut."

Again the woman nodded.

"Okay. Here goes nothing. Just remember I've warned you," Lynx advised her. He slowly removed his palm from her mouth, ready to shut her up if she double-crossed him.

Not a peep came out of her. She regarded him with a mixture of resentment and curiosity.

"What's your name?" Lynx demanded.

"Eleanore. Eleanore DeCoud."

"Well, my name is Lynx. Do you mind tellin' me what you're doing way out here in the boondocks all by your lonesome?"

Apprehension dominated her visage. "Why should I answer you?"

"Because if you don't I'll rip your throat to shreds."

Eleanore blinked, but her resolve stayed firm. "Is that all you think about? Ripping people apart?"

Lynx studied her for a moment, trying to gauge her character. "Look, lady, all I want to do is get to the bottom of this. Here I am, stuck in the middle of a freakin' swamp, cut off from my pals, with jokers in black tryin' to blow me away, and I bump into you. Put yourself in my shoes. Wouldn't you want some answers?"

"You're not wearing shoes," Eleanore noted.

"What difference does it make?" Lynx snapped. "It was a figure of speech, for cryin' out loud."

The woman scrutinized his face, her brow knit in perplexity. "How do I know I can trust you?"

"If I'd wanted to kill you, you'd already be dead," Lynx pointed out to demonstrate his reliability.

"I don't even know what you are!" Eleanore exclaimed. "For all I know, you could be one of the Baron's creatures."

"Who's this Baron?"

"You really don't know?"

Lynx hissed lightly. "Look, bimbo. I don't have time for this crap. My friends are in trouble and I've got to find them, pronto. So you're comin' with me."

"No."

"It wasn't a request, lady," Lynx stated. "You're comin' whether you want to or not." He rose and grasped her right wrist, about to haul her erect.

Eleanore frowned and gazed past him, at the bayou, at the pool to his rear, and her eyes suddenly widened in abject terror. She pointed with her left arm and uttered a strangled shriek.

Suspecting she might be trying to trick him, Lynx twisted his head to look over his right shoulder. The sight he beheld transfixed him with dread.

Rising out of the pool, its scaly body dripping water, its baleful reptilian orbs riveted on them, its huge maw parted to reveal its glistening teeth, was an enormous alligator.

CHAPTER FIVE

Blade took several strides to the east, intending to rush to Lynx's aid, when Ferret abruptly yelled a warning.

"Blade! To the south!"

The Warrior swung around and saw a half-dozen men dressed all in black charging toward the cabin. Each man held a weapon, either a rifle, an assault rifle, or submachine gun, and the expressions on their faces were anything but friendly. Blade whipped the Thompson up, worked the cocking handle, and fired a short burst, gratified at seeing three of the figures drop.

"More to the north, yes!" Gremlin shouted.

Both hybrids cut loose with their AR-15's.

Gunfire erupted all around them, coming from every direction, the rounds smacking into the ground or thudding into the cabin walls.

Blade backpedaled, glancing eastward again, and discovered over a dozen of the uniformed forms coming through the weeds, far too many to try and take head-on. The three of them were drastically outnumbered and the enemy had the element of surprise. Under such circumstances only one option was viable. Retreat. "Back the way we came!" he commanded, loosing a hail of lead at the onrushing men.

"What about Lynx?" Ferret responded, and shot into the trees to the north.

Blade came to the corner of the structure and ducked behind it, firing all the while. "We'll be back for him!" he bellowed.

"I'm not leaving him!" Ferret declared, sighting on a man in black and dispatching him with a single shot.

"We have no choice!" Blade cried. "Now move it!"

Both Ferret and Gremlin, displaying obvious reluctance, backed to the relative shelter of the north wall, where they were screened from the figures to the east and south.

"On me!" Blade directed, and ran westward as five or six bullets smacked into the wood near his head. He bent down as he sprinted to minimize his profile, and he was almost to the northwest corner when he saw four more foes emerging from the trees 40 yards distant, two white men and two blacks.

Damn.

The Warrior pressed the stock to his right shoulder and aimed high to compensate for the range, then squeezed the trigger. The model he used had been fitted with a Cutts compensator and a superior-quality Lyman rearsight by the Family Gunsmiths, ensuring exceptional accuracy in the hands of a seasoned combat veteran. And when it came to warfare, Blade had more experience than most men alive. He mowed the quartet down just as they were bringing their weapons to bear. "Let's go," he prompted, and sped toward the woods.

Ferret and Gremlin stayed hard on the giant's heels, providing covering fire to their rear, compelling their mysterious assailants to duck or die.

Blade expected to feel a slug bore into his back at any instant, but he reached the sanctuary of the forest in safety, and spun to protect his companions as they darted in beside him.

The gunfire had ceased.

"I don't like leaving Lynx," Ferret groused.

"Gremlin neither, no."

"Couldn't be helped," Blade said. He distinguished men in black bearing down on them from both sides, and he turned and moved off. "Come on."

"What's your plan?" Ferret inquired, complying.

"We'll play it by ear."

"That's a terrific plan," Ferret snapped. "Alexander the Great would be proud of you."

"Do you have a better idea?" Blade asked. He vaulted a log in his path and bore to the south.

"Yeah. We should have gone after Lynx."

"How? They had us cut off."

"We could have mowed the bastards down," Ferret proposed.

"Or they might have mowed us down," Blade countered. "We can't help Lynx if we're dead."

"Good point, yes," Gremlin said.

Blade moved rapidly, repeatedly looking to their rear to check for signs of pursuit. His mind whirled with dozens of questions. Who were those guys in black? Why had those men attacked without warning? What connection did they have with the party who had sent the plea for aid? Were they the *reason* the message had been sent?

"Does this happen on all your missions?" Ferret inquired.

"What?"

"Does everything usually go wrong right off the bat? I mean, we're not here an hour and we've got some jerks we don't even know trying to riddle us with holes."

The Warrior went around a thicket and started up a low knoll. "Yeah," he said, staring behind them yet again. "You've heard of Murphy's Law, I take it?"

"Who hasn't?"

"I bet you didn't know that Murphy is my second cousin."

Lynx grinned. "No, I didn't. That explains a lot."

"Excuse Gremlin, yes?" the humanoid interjected. "Gremlin thought Murphy is make-believe, no?"

"He is," Blade said.

"Then how—?" Gremlin began, and fell silent when a loud whistle sounded from 20 or 30 yards to the north.

Blade reached the crest of the knoll and halted. He squatted in the cover of a verdant bush and scanned their back trail. The hybrids did likewise, one on either side.

"I can hear them," Ferret disclosed.

"Gremlin too, yes!" Gremlin stated.

"They're well north of us and heading in the wrong direction," Ferret detailed, his head cocked to the right as he listened intently.

"Dumbbells, no?" Gremlin commented, and snickered.

"There must be dozens of them," Blade said, calculating the odds and planning their stategy. "We need to know who they are and why they're trying to kill us."

Ferret smiled in anticipation. "We capture one?"

"We capture one," Blade confirmed. "You two lead the way. Your hearing is superior to mine. If we can snatch a straggler, we'll persuade him to give us information."

"What if he doesn't want to cooperate, yes?" Gremlin asked.

Blade's voice became hard, almost raspy. "He'll cooperate."

"Let's get cracking," Ferret suggested. "For all we know Lynx could be in their hands by now."

"Lynx never let himself be captured, no," Gremlin averred.

"He let himself be captured by the Doktor, didn't he?" Ferret responded.

"Yes," Gremlin acknowledged.

"And he got himself caught by the Superiors, didn't he?"

Gremlin gazed to the north. "Let's get cracking, yes?"

Blade let the others advance several yards before he fell in. He reflected on Gremlin's peculiar mode of speech, a consequence of operations the Doktor had performed on the humanoid's brain. The sagacious Family leader, Plato, believed the Doktor had been conducting experiments on the area of the brain called the cerebral cortex, the part concerned with such complex mental processes as speech and thought. Somehow, the Doktor's tampering had altered Gremlin's ability to use proper syntax in his verbal communications. Periodically the condition went into a degree of remission and Gremlin would speak in an almost-normal manner. At other times, and for no apparent reason whatsoever, Gremlin's speech would deteriorate dramatically.

Ferret led them to the northwest at a cautious pace, his short, wiry body navigating the rough terrain with deceptive ease, a fluidity of motion only Lynx or another bestial hybrid could hope to match.

Gremlin, while able to proceed with consummate stealth, lacked the acrobatic finesse of his diminutive friend.

Compared to them, and even with years of experience under his belt, Blade felt like a novice in the art of silent stalking. He'd never admit as much to them, and he resolved to improve until he was their virtual equal.

The forest presented a dense web of luxuriant vegetation of every type and description. Insects buzzed and flitted from plant to plant. The earlier gunfire had caused the wildlife to fall collectively silent, and the quietude of the birds and larger animals lent an eerie, somber quality to the landscape.

Blade used the opportunity to replace the partially expended magazine in the Thompson with a full one. The 30-round detachable box-type magazines were easy to eject and insert, and he drove the fresh one home with a forceful slap. The rugged performance of the Thompson had impressed him so far. Perhaps, if the gun continued to live up to its prewar reputation, he would consider using it on other missions. He liked the heavily ribbed barrel and the wooden buttstock. To an average man the submachine gun might be a bit heavy; to someone of his massive size the Thompson had the weight of a toy.

Several oak trees appeared 50 feet ahead of them.

Ferret suddenly flattened and motioned for them to do the same.

Blade dropped and saw the reason.

A thin black man, garbed in the dapper black uniform, stepped into sight from behind one of the trees and surveyed his surroundings. He clutched an Ingram MAC10 sub-machine gun fitted with a two-position shoulder piece and a webstrap.

The Warrior trained the Thompson on the man, just in case they were spotted. But his concern proved unfounded as the man in black rotated to the north and stood there studying the woods. Why did they wear those mirrored sunglasses? Blade mused. To conceal their eyes so an enemy would never know in which direction they were actually looking? If so, whoever they worked for must be very clever.

Ferrat laid his AR-15 down and gestured at Gremlin, and together they crawled toward the man in black.

Blade could do nothing but wait. He admired the skill the pair displayed, a testimony to the fact they had been created to function as perfect assassins. He scrutinized the trees on all sides, puzzled by the presence of just one foe. Where were the rest? Were there other men stationed at regular intervals?

The black man coughed lightly and cradled the MAC10 under his right arm. He stretched, arching his back, and turned in a complete circle.

The hybrids froze in unison, their bodies flush with the ground, blending in with the grass and brush.

Evidently satisfied that he wasn't in any danger, the man leaned against a trunk and stared idly to the west. He yawned and shook his head vigorously.

Blade noted the last act with interest. Had the ambushers been awake for an extended period, waiting for someone in particular, or had they been there waiting to see if anyone would show up in response to the distress call? The trap had been thorough, and probably Lynx heading east along the trail had caused them to close in prematurely.

Ferret and Gremlin were within 30 feet of the trees.

The Warrior felt a twinge of pain in his left side. Some months back he had been shot and sustained a terrible wound, and any strenuous exertion still aggravated it. The discomfort made him think of his precious Jenny. She had extracted the bullet herself, doing a superb job even though she had to improvise and use a screwdriver for a probe. In another four or five months he should be as good as new.

Thinking about the wound also brought to mind all the other injuries he had sustained since becoming a Warrior. At the rate he was going, what with all the bullet holes, cut and slash marks, teeth and claw imprints, and sundry other scars, he'd be lucky to have a square inch of unmarred skin by the time he retired from the Warrior ranks. If he lived that long.

Twenty feet separated the hybrids from the man in black.

Blade forced himself to stop thinking about his lovely wife, and concentrated on covering the mutations. Of late his mental discipline had been more lax than was usually the case, and he determined to work on his self-control at every chance.

Ferret and Gremlin had now diverged, Ferret moving to the right, the humanoid to the left. The grass scarcely stirred as they advanced. Thanks to the Doktor's manipulation of their genetic codes, they were the ultimate development in the lethal arts, living liquidators par excellence.

Blade sighted down the Thompson, then stiffened when he detected motion underneath the barrel. The next moment something began crawling up his naked forearm, and he glanced down to behold a spider the size of his fist clinging to his skin. Goose bumps broke out all over his flesh and he almost flung his arm out to dislodge the arachnid. To do so, however, might alert the man in black to the fact others were nearby, might give Ferret and Gremlin away, so he gritted his teeth and remained motionless.

The spider, with a rust color and sporting a peculiar orange design on its back near its multiple eyes, climbed in a leisurely fashion, its hairy legs rising and falling slowly.

Was it toxic?

The mere thought served to make Blade tingle all over. He watched the spider inch upward, then looked at the hybrids to mark their progress. They were drawing steadily nearer to the guy in the sunglasses, and soon they would be within pouncing range. At that point they would be the most vulnerable and be dependent on him to down the man if necessary. But how could he fire with the spider perched on his arm? The slightest movement could prompt the arachnid to bite.

The spider stopped five inches from his left palm.

Blade scarcely breathed. If the arachnid stayed on his arm much longer, he'd be forced to make a decision that could cost him his life. He glanced at Ferret and Gremlin and saw them suddenly spring toward the figure next to the tree.

Just as the man turned in their direction.

CHAPTER
SIX

For several heartbeats Lynx stood transfixed by the terrifying sight, until a sharp cry roused him from his astonishment.

Eleanore screamed.

Lynx roughly hauled her erect and shoved, sending her into the weeds to the north. He followed, backpedaling, watching the armored leviathan lumber up the bank and bear down on them, its thick, short legs pumping, its tail weaving from side to side.

"Oh, God!" Eleanore wailed, fleeing in abject horror.

How fast could alligators run? Lynx wondered as he raced after her.

The broad, rounded snout of the gator parted the vegetation as the reptile barreled toward them, moving at a surprisingly swift pace.

Lynx stayed on the woman's heels. They had a 12-foot lead and were gaining ground slowly, but 12 feet didn't seem like very much at all when a creature akin to a prehistoric dinosaur was in hot pursuit. He estimated their pursuer to be a whopping 18 feet in length, a promordial colossus capable of rending him in half with one swipe of its wicked teeth.

Eleanore stumbled but kept going without breaking her stride

Alarmed that she might indeed trip, Lynx concentrated on her movements, ready to assist at the first hint of trouble. If the woman did go down, he would be compelled to defend her, and he entertained grave reservations over whether his nails could inflict much damage on the alligator's tough reptilian hide. Even using the AR-15—

The asault rifle!

Lynx suddenly realized he had foolishly left the weapon lying somewhere near the pool. Now all he had to rely on were his nails and his teeth; against this bestial denizen of the swamp they hardly seemed enough. He looked over his left shoulder and almost laughed in relief.

The alligator had stopped and was simply standing there, balefully regarding their flight.

Wary that the reptile would renew its charge, Lynx kept his eyes on the animal until they were at least 30 yards away and he could no longer see the creature. "You can stop now," he said.

Eleanore seemed not to hear him. She gasped for air, her legs driving hard, swatting at the bushes that clawed at her clothing.

"You can stop, bimbo," Lynx repeated, and batted her on the left shoulder.

Startled, Eleanore slowed down and glanced at him, then to their rear. "Where is it?"

"Takin' a dump."

"What?" Eleanore asked, not quite comprehending. She halted and peered to the south. "It's gone?"

"That's what I've been tryin' to tell you, lady."

"I've got a name, you know."

"Good for you," Lynx snapped, surveying the field around them. "I don't see any sign of those bozos in black, but I don't feel safe here what with Tyrannosaurus rex just waitin' for a chance to nip our tootsies."

Eleanore regarded him quizzically. "Tie-ranny-who?"

"Tyrannosaurus rex, a dinosaur. A big buddy told me all about them."

"Never heard of them. Are you sure you know what you're talking about?"

"What?"

"Everybody and their grandmother knows the animal we saw is called an alligator. Maybe the folks where you come from call them tie-rannies, but in these parts we just call them gators."

Lynx smirked and shook his head. "Yep. No doubt about it."

"About what?"

"The fact you're a bimbo."

"Stop calling me that!"

"What are you going to do if I don't? Stamp your foot?" Lynx cracked, and took hold of her left wrist.

"Leave go of me," Eleanore protested, and tugged, striving to break free.

"Don't start again," Lynx warned. He headed westward, hauling her along, and made for an expanse of woodland 70 yards distant.

"You're awful strong for such a little thing," Eleanore remarked.

"And mean too, lady. Mean enough to break your arm if you give me any grief."

"Didn't you tell me your name is Lynx?"

"Wow. I'm impressed. You can remember something for more than two seconds. Maybe you're not a bimbo after all."

"I wish you'd stop insulting me."

"Can't help myself," Lynx said. "It's been a lousy day so far, and bumpin' into you hasn't made matters much better."

"What are you doing here? Where are you from?"

"I'll ask the questions."

Eleanore frowned and studied his feline visage. "I don't

know what to make of you."

Lynx didn't bother to respond. He gazed to the northwest, trying to spot the cabin, but a stand of trees blocked his view.

"I mean, you certainly don't act like one of the Baron's creatures."

"There's that name again. Who is the Baron?"

"He's the *houngan*."

Lynx glanced at her. "The what?"

"The high priest."

"High priest? Is he some kind of religious yo-yo?"

"You really don't know, do you?"

"I wouldn't ask if I did."

Lines creased Eleanore's forehead as she pondered for several seconds. "All right," she finally declared. "I believe you're not connected to Baron Laveau. No one could pretend to be as dumb as you are."

"Thanks, twit."

"I'm not trying to bad-mouth you."

"You could've fooled me."

Eleanore glared at him. "Why are you always so hostile?"

"Maybe because I learned an important lesson when I was knee-high to a kitten."

"A lesson?"

"Yeah. I learned that the world will stomp you into the dust unless you stomp back. Life is hard, lady. Most humans don't give a damn about anything but themselves, and they hate hybrids like me with a passion. The only exceptions I've ever met are the sicky-sweets at the Home."

"I don't understand. Who are the sicky-sweets?"

"Never mind."

They covered 20 yards before Eleanore spoke again.

"I want to know the truth. Are you going to hurt me?"

"Only if you don't cooperate. I'm fixin' to take you to Jumbo."

"Who?"

"You'll see. He'll know what to do with you."

"Where is he?"

"That's what I'd like to know. We've got to find him and my other friends."

"You *have* friends?"

"Keep it up, lady."

"I'm just trying to make sense of what you say. It's not easy. You talk in riddles."

"Don't strain your brain on my account."

Eleanore expelled a sharp breath in frustration. "You're impossible. Do you know that?"

"You sound like my wife," Lynx said, and nearly fell when the woman halted so abruptly that she wrenched on his arm and caused him to stumble. "What the hell do you think you're doing?" he demanded angrily.

"Did I hear you correctly? Are you married?" Eleanore inquired, her features reflecting her shock at the revelation.

"Yeah. I've got a main squeeze. Her name is Melody. So what?"

Eleanore roved her eyes from his head to his toes. "But you're a—a—whatever you are? How could any woman marry you?"

A shadow seemed to descend on Lynx and his countenance hardened. "Oh. Is that it. You can't imagine how a freak like me could have a wife?"

"I didn't mean to imply—" Eleanore began, but the hybrid never gave her a chance to finish the sentence.

"Screw you, bimbo," Lynx stated harshly, and resumed walking toward the forest.

"I don't think you're a freak," Eleanore declared. "But you have to admit you're different."

Lynx stalked forward without replying.

"Listen to me, damn you!"

"Save your breath, bigot."

Eleanore dug in her heels and tried to wrench her wrist loose. "I am *not* a bigot!" she protested. "I can't help it if I don't know how to relate to you without hurting your oversensitive feelings. I've never met anything like you before. The only other mutations I've seen are those from the swamps, those the Baron has collected at his estate. He puts them in cages and gets his kicks by tormenting them, by poking them with red-hot irons and whipping them. Things like two-headed black bears or bobcats with three eyes. He's the one who can't stand freaks.''

Lynx digested the information inscrutably. ''The Baron does this, huh?''

''Yeah. And lots worse.''

''Then I'll have to pay him a visit before I head back to the Home.''

''Forget it.''

''Why?''

''You wouldn't get two feet past the outer walls. His estate is guarded by the *tonton macoutes* and other things. And there's always Damballah.''

''Who's that?''

''Damballah isn't a person,'' Eleanore said, and glanced nervously at the weeds enclosing them. ''Damballah is the Snake God.''

''Let me get this straight. The Baron worships a snake?''

''Baron Laveau is the high priest of the Black Snake Society. The *houmfor* is located behind his estate. It's also guarded day and night.''

''What the devil is a *houmfor*?''

''The temple where the rites are practiced, where Damballah is summoned.''

Lynx stared into her eyes. ''And you're not makin' any of this nonsense up? There really are humans who go around worshiping some dinky snake?''

''Damballah isn't dinky. Damballah is the mother and father of all snakes combined in one serpent. Damballah rules New Orleans.''

''A snake rules the city?'' Lynx said, and laughed.

''It's no laughing matter. Damballah rules through the Baron and Majesta.''

''What's Majesta? An earthworm?'' Lynx queried, snickering at his joke.

"No, dummy. Majesta is the *mambo,* the high priestess. She's just as depraved as the Baron, maybe more so," Eleanore disclosed bitterly.

"You don't sound too fond of either of them."

"I hate them!" Eleanore declared. "Why do you think I joined the Resistance? I want to see the Baron and Majesta destroyed. I want to help free the people of New Orleans from the Black Snake Society. The horror has to end!"

Lynx was surprised and impressed by the intensity of her passion. She genuinely despised the Black Snake Society, which qualified her as one of the good guys. Blade had provided a briefing on the distress call received at the Home, and he'd related the pertinent fact that the caller had specifically mentioned the Black Snake Society as being the group that had control of New Orleans. "Tell me more about the Black Snake Society," he prompted.

"I can tell you everything you need to know in one word," Eleanore said.

Lynx stared skeptically at her. "One measly word?"

"Yep."

"What is this magical word?"

"Voodoo."

CHAPTER
SEVEN

In a twinkling Blade decided on his course of action. He couldn't stand idly by and let Ferret or Gremlin be killed, not even with a potentially toxic spider clinging to his forearm. So at the same instant the guy in black pivoted, Blade raised the Thompson and fired. But his sacrifice, as it turned out, was unnecessary.

No sooner had the man started to rotate than Ferret executed a prodigious leap, and just as the man in black completed his revolution, before he could hope to react, Ferret alighted with all the force of a furry cannonball.

The startled object of the hybrid's attack could do no more than utter an astounded gasp and try to bring his MAC10 into play.

Ferret wouldn't let him. Snarling deep in his throat, Ferret batted the Ingram aside with his left arm and sank the nails on his right hand into the man's shoulder.

Gremlin was also in motion. Less than a second after Ferret hit their adversary high, causing the man to stumble rearward, Gremlin took the man low, hitting him below the knees, wrapping his arms around the man's legs and driving forward in a timely tackle.

The guy in black went down with the hybrids on top.

Blade saw all of this transpire even as he braced for the anticipated spider bite. He focused on the arachnid, feeling its hairy legs rubbing on his skin, elated to see it going down his arm instead of up. In another few seconds it would drop to the ground and he could go aid the hybrids.

Not that they needed any help.

Ferret and Gremlin made short work of their opponent. The mammalian hybrid tore the MAC10 from the man's grasp, then clamped his right hand on the man's throat. The humanoid delivered a smashing blow to the midsection that made the man sputter and wheeze and effectively nipped all resistance in the bud. Working together, each taking an arm, Ferret and Gremlin yanked their vanquished enemy erect and headed toward the Warrior.

Blade watched them approach, still loathe to move until the spider took its leave. The arachnid had halted an inch from his elbow and appeared in no particular hurry to vacate its newfound home.

Of all the dumb luck!

Ferret and Gremlin hastened over, supporting the man in black between them, the MAC10 dangling from Ferret's left hand.

"Good job," Blade commented, looking up.

"If you don't mind my saying so, this is a hell of a time to be taking a nap," Ferret cracked.

"Nice of you to help us, yes?" Gremlin added.

"Do either of you know anything about spiders?" Blade casually inquired, staying perfectly still.

"They're uglier than Lynx. That's all I know," Ferret replied.

"And they have a better disposition, no?" Gremlin said.

"Why do you ask?" Ferret questioned the Warrior.

Blade nodded at his left arm. "I was hoping one of you could tell me whether my new pet is poisonous."

The hybrids glanced down.

"Damn!" Ferret blurted out.

"Don't move, yes?" Gremlin advised.

"Wouldn't think of it," Blade assured them.

The man in black was struggling to break free, but his strength amounted to virtually nothing when compared to the combined might of the hybrids, beings who had been genetically bred to possess the power of any three ordinary men. He spied the arachnid and ceased struggling to voice an exclamation. "*Mon Dieu!*"

"What did he say?" Ferret queried.

"I don't know, no," Gremlin answered. He leaned down a few inches, studying the spider. "Do you want me to flick it off, yes?"

"I don't want to touch it," Blade said. "If we wait a minute or two, it's bound to go somewhere else."

"You hope," Ferret remarked.

Abruptly, from the north, came a harsh shout. "Corporal Pétion?"

The prisoner promptly responded. "Je—!"

Gremlin whipped his left fist down and in, planting another punch in their prisoner's stomach, doubling the man in half and rendering him temporarily incapable of yelling again.

But the harm had already been done.

"What was that? Where are you?" a man called out.

"This way!" cried another. "*Je pense.*"

Blade listened intently to the language being used. He recognized the last two as French words from lessons taken during his schooling years at the Home, brief lessons encompassing only four months and merely intended as an introduction to the language. Why were the men in black speaking both English and a little French? English, as far as he knew, had been the official language in New Orleans before the war. Did it have something to do with the Cajuns and the Creoles?

"We've got to get out of here," Ferret declared.

"I couldn't agree more," Blade concurred, and stared at the spider. Enough was enough. He couldn't afford to wait any longer. Still holding the Thompson with his left hand, he released the trigger and brought his right hand over to his immobile forearm. He drew back his middle finger and let fly, his nail connecting with the spider's side and flicking the arachnid over a foot.

Straight at Ferret, who adroitly dodged the kicking projectile. "Hey! Watch where you're flicking your spiders!"

Blade grinned and shoved to his feet. "Let's go."

"What about this guy, yes?" Gremlin asked. "He'll slow us down, no?"

"No," Blade answered, and stepped forward to deliver a right uppercut to the tip of the man's chin. The prisoner sagged, and would have fallen if not supported by the hybrids. "Give him to me," Blade directed, and crouched so they could drape the now-unconscious man over his right shoulder.

"You're going to carry this guy all by yourself?" Ferret inquired doubtfully as he let go.

"Yep," the giant replied, and straightened.

"He's at least one hundred and seventy pounds, no?" Gremlin noted.

"I can use the exercise," Blade told them. He faced to the south and ran.

"If you get tired we'll take over," Ferret offered.

"Thanks, but I can manage," Blade said.

They covered the terrain rapidly, vaulting logs and skirting thickets with deceptive ease, heading deeper into the forest, bearing to the south. Several minutes elasped. To their rear, growing fainter and fainter, were the yells of the ambushers.

Blade jogged for almost ten minutes, until he was convinced they had put enough distance between them to preclude the possibility of being overtaken. He came to a small clearing and halted. "I think we've lost them," he said.

"Gremlin agree," the humanoid mentioned.

"Then we'll take a break and question our captive," Blade stated.

Ferret started sniffing the air. "I smell water. Close. Real close."

"We'll check it out," Blade proposed. "Lead the way."

Demonstrating the unerring instincts of his bestial inheritance, Ferret led them 15 yards farther and stopped at the top of a sloping bank.

Below them stretched a marshy tract, part of the bayou visible from the air. Intermittent small islands, consisting of wet, spongy mounds overgrown with trees and dense undergrowth, dotted the lily-choked surface of the water. Cranes, ducks, and other waterfowl could be seen going about their daily routines. Here and there the tall reeds moved, stirred by creatures lurking in the swamp.

"Nice place for a vacation," Ferret said.

Blade deposited his burden on the bank. He leaned down to remove the man's sunglasses, and discovered the temple pieces were attached to an elastic black band, which explained why the glasses hadn't fallen off when the man had been slugged. Blade slipped the band off the left temple piece, pulled off the sunglasses, and straightened.

"What are you going to do with those, yes?" Gremlin queried.

"Toss them."

"Gremlin would like them, please."

"Be my guest," Blade said, and handed them over.

"What do you want them for?" Ferret asked his friend.

"What else, no?" Gremlin rejoined, and donned the mirrored lenses, carefully reattaching the elastic band to ensure the glasses would stay in place. He lowered his arms and grinned. "What do you think?"

"I think you look like a space alien," Blade commented.

"Gremlin never heard of them, no."

"I saw pictures of them in an old magazine in our library," the giant related. "Actually, they were an artist's rendering of space aliens people claimed to have seen. With the shape of your head and those dark glasses, you look just like an alien."

"What was the name of the magazine, yes?"

"I believe it was called *UFO.*"

"Gremlin would like to read it when we get back. Gremlin has always believed there is intelligent life on other planets."

Ferret snickered. "There sure isn't any on this planet."

The prisoner groaned and rolled over onto his back.

"Time to play Forty Questions," Blade said. He knelt and drew his right Bowie, then held the gleaming blade directly over the black man's right eye.

A few moments later the captive awakened and automatically tried to rise. His dark eyes widened to the size of walnuts when he beheld the sharpened steel tip of the Bowie, and he froze.

"Hi there," Blade said amiably. "We need some answers."

The prisoner swallowed, licked his lips, and replied in a strange tongue.

Blade waited patiently until the man finished. "I don't understand your language. Speak English."

Again the prisoner spoke in the peculiar language.

"Listen closely," Blade told him coldly. "I won't repeat this." He paused. "I suspect that you're playing us for fools. You know English, probably almost as well as I do. So if you don't tell me what I want to know, right this second, I will bury this knife in your socket." He paused once more for effect. "Now tell us your name."

The answer was immediately forthcoming. "Henri Pétion. And yes, I speak English perfectly. I should. It's the most common language."

"Henri," Blade repeated. "It sounds French."

"My ancestors were Haitian," Pétion revealed in a tone that implied the revelation explained everything.

The Warrior mentally envisioned a globe kept in the Family library, its representation of the world somewhat faded after decades of steady use. "If memory serves, isn't Haiti an island in the West Indies?"

Pétion nodded.

"And your ancestors moved to New Orleans?"

"Oui. Many years before the big war."

Blade snatched at the black shirt with his left hand. "What's with the uniform?"

"I am one of the *tonton macoutes,"* Pétion declared proudly, almost arrogantly.

"The what?"

"The magicians."

Perplexed, Blad looked at the hybrids, who were viewing the interrogation with interest, then back down at their prisoner. "I don't get it. Are you saying you practice some form of magic?"

"Oui. One day I will move up in rank from a *tonton macoute* to a *boko,* a sorcerer. Perhaps, many years from now, I may even become the *houngan* of our *houmfor."*

"Whoa. Slow down," Blade stated. "You're getting ahead of me. What's a *houngan*?"

"A high priest."

"In what?"

"The Black Snake Society."

The Warrior recalled the information given by the party who had placed the distress call, and his gray eyes narrowed. "I've heard that the Black Snake Society controls New Orleans."

"Oui, and for many miles around," Pétion said with his haughty air. "The invincible magic of the Black Snake Society has made us the masters."

"Wait a minute," Ferret interjected. "What's all this bull about magic? This guy must be an idiot if he believes in such mumbo jumbo."

Pétion glared at the hybrid. "Voodoo is not mumbo jumbo," he snapped, emphasizing the last two words distastefully. 'Voodoo is the way."

Ferret laughed.

"Mock me all you want, animal. But I will have the last

laugh. I will use voodoo to call on the spirit world, and you will die a horrible death for scoffing at the true way.''

"I'm trembling in fear," Ferret said.

Pétion's voice rose shrilly. "I will call on Damballah, and our god will come to slay you in the night. You will be consumed alive and suffer the torments of Hell.''

"Don't get your hopes up, turkey.''

Blade noticed unchecked fury contorting Pétion's features, and he concluded the man firmly believed in whatever magic was practiced. He'd heard about voodoo many years ago, but his knowledge of the religion was scant. He opened his mouth to probe further into the matter.

From behind them, from the bayou, issued a sibilant hissing.

CHAPTER EIGHT

"What in the world is voo-boo?" Lynx asked.

"It's *voodoo*, dummy. A religion to many people, a religion laced with sorcery, a religion where powerful spirit forces control the lives of everyday people," Eleanore detailed. "There's good voodoo and there's bad voodoo, and by bad voodoo I mean the dark side where black magic is practiced."

Lynx considered her words for a few seconds. "So this Black Snake Society is a voodoo cult?"

Eleanore nodded. "From what I've learned, the Black Snake Society got its start many years ago, way before the war. It was just one of several secret voodoo societies in the United States, based right here in New Orleans. After the world almost came to an end, after the government fell apart, the Black Snake Society grew stronger and stronger. Then, when Damballah appeared, they were able to take control of this whole region."

"Hold it. Are you tellin' me their snake god actually appeared to them? Showed up as flesh and blood?"

"Yep. Damballah disposed of all their enemies for them,

one by one, and before too long the Black Snake Society ruled the entire city.''

''And people have actually seen this snake god?'' Lynx inquired in disbelief.

''Quite a few. Just the other night I was talking to a man who saw it.''

''Amazing,'' was all Lynx could think to say. He headed for the trees again, pulling her along. ''Wait until Blade hears this.''

''Who's this Blade?''

''A pal of mine. We're here to close the Black Snake Society down.''

''Then we're on the same side!''

''We are if you're tellin' the truth.''

Eleanore tried to stop but he yanked her forward. ''Are you calling me a liar?''

''There's always that possibility.''

''But I've been perfectly honest with you.''

The hybrid glanced at her. ''How do I know that? Until I have more proof, I'm treatin' you like I would any bimbo who might haul off and stab me in the back.''

''Will you *please* stop calling me that?''

Lynx smirked. ''Why not? I'm gettin' tired of you nagging me.'' He stared thoughtfully at her. ''If you want to earn my trust, you can start by tellin' me why you were traipsing around in the middle of a friggin' swamp.''

''I've been sneaking around for almost two days trying to evade being captured by the *tonton macoutes*. The night before last I came out here with another member of the Resistance, a guy named Jerry Price. We were bringing supplies to Adrien Dessalines, our radio operator.''

''The Resistance has a radio?'' Lynx asked innocently to elicit more information.

''Yep. A shortwave radio.'' Eleanore frowned. ''At least we *did* have one. Somehow the Baron found out about our operation. He was waiting for us with a bunch of his goons. Jerry drew his knife and tried to stab Laveau, but the *tonton macoutes* were all over him like barracuda on a minnow. They pinned him down and disarmed him, then held him down while the Baron kicked him a few times just for the hell of it."

A strange scent reached Lynx and he sniffed the air in an attempt to identify the source. Distracted, he covered ten yards before the significance of her statements occurred to him. He regarded her suspiciously, then faced front to avoid alerting her. "How is it that you managed to get away?" he casually asked.

"I was just lucky, I guess. Two of the *tonton macoutes* grabbed me, but when Jerry pulled his survival knife they let me go and pounced on him. None of them paid any attention to me while they were fighting Jerry, so I took advantage of it and ran."

"And you were able to elude them. My compliments."

Eleanore detected a slight tinge of sarcasm in his tone, which puzzled her. "It wasn't easy. They took off after me. Thank God it was night. In broad daylight they would have easily caught me. As it was, I just barely escaped them."

"Lucky you."

"You don't know the half of it. Anyway, I hid in this thicket until they called off the search and went back to the cabin where Adrien had been doing his broadcasting. I snuck to within twenty yards of the front door and saw the Baron and some of his goons taking Jerry, Adrien, and the short-wave."

"They didn't keep hunting you?"

"I was surprised too. I guess the Baron didn't figure I was much of a threat. Maybe he figured hunger would make me give up. I haven't eaten since. Besides, they posted guards at the boats, and there's no way anyone can make it through the bayou without one. There's too many gators and snakes and other things. Horrible things."

Lynx walked in silence for the next 30 feet, contemplating her disclosure and striving to decide whether he could count her as an ally or an enemy. Although she sounded sincere, any accomplished liar could do so and maintain a straight face. Personally, he wanted to believe her. But her story contained a few glaring inconsistencies. For instance, how likely was it that the *tonton* whatever-they-were would up and release her when there must have been enough of them on hand to deal with the other members of the Resistance? And how feasible was her assertion that she had eluded her pursuers when she'd had maybe 60 seconds head start at the most? Another objection presented itself. "How did the Baron know about the cabin?"

"I wish I knew."

"Sounds to me like he knew all about your shortwave and set a neat little trap."

"That's the way I read it."

"And you have no idea how he knew?"

Eleanore glanced at the hybrid. "I told you I don't. Why do you keep asking?"

"No reason."

"Liar. You don't believe me, do you?"

"Sure I do."

"No, you don't."

Again the peculiar odor tantalized Lynx's nostrils, and he cocked his head, his nose flaring, stumped. What in the world was it? He vaguely recalled having encountered such a scent before.

"Is something wrong?" Eleanore asked, gazing nervously at the forest.

"No."

"Then why were you smelling the air like that?"

"I like to exercise my nose once an hour whether it needs the workout or not."

"Come on. Be honest with me."

"Why should I buck the trend?"

Eleanore clenched her fists, then nodded to herself. "I knew you didn't believe me. Well, screw you. I'm not telling you another damn thing."

"Suit yourself. I'll do my best to survive the shock."

"Has anyone ever told you that you're a smart-ass?"

"Nope. No one."

"There you go lying again. How does your wife put up with you? She must have the patience of a saint."

Lynx abruptly halted and turned. "Keep your mouth off of my squeeze, lady. She's got more class than any ten broads I know."

The fiery passion in the hybrid's eyes subdued Eleanore's anger. "Sorry," she blurted out. "I wasn't trying to insult your woman."

"You'd better not," Lynx warned, and resumed hiking to the west. "And technically speaking, she's not exactly a woman."

"What do you mean?"

"Melody is a hybrid like me. We were bred in test tubes by sons of bitches who were tryin' to play God."

"I never heard of such a thing. What's a test tube?"

"A little glass container shaped like your finger."

"Are you putting me on?"

"Look at me, stupid. Do you think I hatched from an egg? Or came from Mars?"

"I know you didn't come from Mars," Eleanore stated.

"Oh?"

"Yeah. I talked to an oldster once who told me all about this book that his grandfather had told him about. It was all about the war between Earth and Mars."

Lynx stopped again, his brow creased in confusion. "What are you babbling about?"

"So you don't know everything, huh? I'm surprised you haven't heard about the war. It took place a couple of hundred years ago. Started in a country called England."

"Mars and the Earth never fought a war, you dingbat."

"Says you. I prefer to believe the oldster. He supplied all the details he remembered. How the Martians came to Earth in these cylinders that resembled meteors, and how they landed in England and wiped out thousands of people with their death rays. They built these huge machines and roamed the land wiping out the population. According to the old man, the Martians nearly ruled the world.''

"Do you expect me to buy this fairy tale of yours?''

"I didn't invent the story. The old man heard the details from his grandfather,'' Eleanore reiterated.

"The old man must have been stoned out of his gourd.''

"He was sober.''

"Idiot,'' Lynx muttered, and kept going.

"Listen to the history expert. How many books on history have you read?''

"None, but—'' Lynx began.

"Then how do you know it's not the truth?''

"If it was, you'd think more folks would know about a war between us and some geeks from Mars. How come I haven't heard about this great war before?''

"No one talks about it much anymore. Why should they? Everyone with half a brain knows it happened.''

"Bet me.''

"And they weren't geeks from Mars. They were octopuses from Mars.''

"Octopuses!'' Lynx exploded in exasperation, and inadvertently released her wrist. "You mean those things in the ocean with all the tentacles?''

"Yep.''

"Let me tell you something, sister. That old man saw you coming a mile off and decided to jerk your G-string. You almost had me believing you until now. Octopuses from Mars!'' Lynx snorted contemptuously, grabbed her arm, and stalked in the direction of the treeline.

"Check with somebody else if you don't believe me.''

"If you think I'm going to waltz up to someone else and ask them if this planet was ever invaded by a bunch of geek octopuses from Mars, you're crazy.''

"Find the book. Then you'll know I told you the truth.''

Lynx thought of the enormous Family library with its hundreds of thousands of volumes stocked by the Founder of the Home, Kurt Carpenter, and speculated on whether the book she mentioned might be included. Carpenter had accumulated half a million books, shelf after shelf of reference books, history books, geography books, books on military tactics, books on gardening, hunting, and fishing. Blade had told Lynx that the library contained the greatest collection in existence, including all the classics, humorous books, scientific tomes, photographic volumes, and many, many more. He had taken the giant's word for it. Lynx wasn't much of a reader, primarily because he could seldom sit still long enough to finish an entire book.

"And here I thought you were Mr. Know-It-All," Eleanore remarked scornfully.

"Not that I believe your garbage for a second, but you've got me curious. Whatever happened to all these invader octopuses? There's none around now."

"They were all killed off by germs."

"Great. Here we go again."

"I'm serious. Do you know how when you have a cold and you cough, you spread all these tiny germs in the air?"

"I know you've got a germ for a brain."

"Look do you want to know the answer or not?"

Lynx sighed. "Sure. Why not? I've listened to this much B.S. Why not give me the rest of it?"

"Okay. The old man told me that the germs in our atmosphere killed the Martians because they don't have the same kind of germs on their planet as we do on ours. So germs that would just affect you and me with a sore throat or a runny nose will wipe out a Martian."

"That's some imagination you've got there, sweetcheeks. One of these days you should write a book of your own. Call it *War of the Geeks.*"

"What's with you and geeks?" Eleanore asked, then did a double take. "Hey. What did you just call me?"

"I don't remember."

"Yes you do. You called me sweetcheeks."

"Don't take it personally. I call chipmunks sweetcheeks, too," Lynx told her. They were now 20 feet from the woods, and for the third time his sensitive nose registered the unknown scent. Only this time the odor sparked a memory. "Do you have pigs in Louisiana?"

"Wild pigs, you mean?"

"I smell pig," Lynx declared. "I don't know if it's wild or tame."

"There wouldn't be any domestic pigs here," Eleanore stated, and suddenly her visage reflected budding shock. "Oh, no!"

Lynx drew up short and glanced at her. "Oh no, what?"

"Boars. A lot of wild boars have spread across the bayous since the war."

A flash of chilling insight electrified the hybrid, and he looked at the gloomy forest just as a 400-pound mass of primal fury hurtled from the undergrowth directly at them, its nine-inch upswept tusks glinting wickedly in the bright sunlight.

CHAPTER NINE

Blade rotated on his heels and stared at the bayou. He expected to see a water snake, perhaps even a cottonmouth, swimming near the bank. Instead, to his utter consternation, he beheld a literal monster of incredible dimensions, a reptile that dwarfed every animal he had ever seen, a creature that rivaled the dinosaurs.

A gargantuan black snake.

The serpent was over 50 yards from the shore, yet even at that distance its tremendous, sinuous bulk eclipsed everything around it, even trees. Ten feet in height and 40 feet in length, the snake appeared to be a throwback to the ancient era when gigantic animals ruled the earth. Its elongated head swung from side to side as it wound across the swamp, and its slender red tongue flicked outward repeatedly, testing the air.

"Tell me I'm dreaming!" Ferret breathed in amazement.

"What if it spots us, yes?" Gremlin declared.

"Take cover," Blade directed, and swiveled to reach for their prisoner.

Henri Pétion was already in motion. The sight of the snake

had produced a remarkable transformation in his visage. Sheer joy lit his eyes and he beamed happily. He shoved off the ground as the giant turned toward him, brushing past his captors in a bound and darting down to the edge of the water.

"What the—" Blade began, rising.

"I'll get him," Ferret offered, and took a step forward.

Suddenly Pétion lifted his arms to the heavens and shouted across the water. "Damballah! Mighty Damballah! Your humble servant is here to do your bidding!"

"What the hell is that idiot doing?" Ferret snapped.

"Gremlin doesn't like this, no," the humanoid offered.

Blade saw the huge snake start to stop. "Hit the dirt," he directed, and suited action to his command by turning and diving into the undergrowth. He heard the brush rustle on either side as the hybrids obeyed, then he crawled to the north and covered a minimum of 20 yards before he halted and rose to his knees.

Pétion had stepped a few feet into the water and was now standing motionless, his arms still raised. "Great Damballah! Hear the prayer of your loyal follower!"

The Warrior looked at the serpent and felt his pulse quicken.

Advancing at a slow, winding clip, the snake was approaching the bank, its gaze fixed on the *tonton macoute*.

What was the fool doing? Blade marveled, and eased lower, slightly parting the weeds in front of him so he could witness whatever happened next. Fleeing was out of the question. The serpent would undoubtedly spot them and overtake them within seconds. The smartest recourse was to stay where they were, well hidden, until the snake departed.

"You have blessed me with a visitation, oh wondrous Damballah!" Pétion cried ecstatically.

The man must be insane! Blade reasoned. He slid the Bowie into its sheath and tucked the Thompson against his right side, his finger on the trigger, ready to cut loose. A glance to his right revealed Ferret a yard away; a glance to his left showed Gremlin crouching behind a bushy clump of matted vegetation.

"Magnificent Snake God!" Pétion raved on. "You came in response to my prayer! You came, yet I did not use the Sacred Drum!"

Blade watched in fascination as the reptile neared the man in black. He was astounded by Pétion's behavior. The man acted as if he *knew* the snake!

"Now you will destroy the enemies of our Society," Pétion shouted. "Now you will show them our power!"

The serpent never deviated from its course. When only 15 yards separated it from the voodoo practitioner, the snake stopped and elevated its head an additional four feet above the ground, that scarlet tongue flicking-flicking-flicking.

Pétion waded out until the water reached his knees. He spread his arms out and stared up at the immense creature. "Go find our enemies, oh, mighty Damballah! Seek them out and devour them as you have done so many times in the past! Show them your followers do not worship you in vain."

Blade stayed as rigid as a rock, hardly breathing, dumbfounded by the riveting tableau.

"Wait until the Baron hears of this!" Pétion declared. "Wait until he hears how you have favored me. I will move up quickly now. Why, I wouldn't be surprised to be appointed *boko*. And all thanks to you!"

The living nightmare slid slowly toward the man in black, its dark, obsidian eyes reflecting its soul-less nature.

Henri Pétion performed a sweeping, obsequious bow. "Lord Damballah, I am yours to command! Do with me as you will." He straightened, his arms at his sides.

The Snake God acknowledged the request.

Suddenly sweeping forward, the black serpent's enormous head darted at the expectant human, its maw opening wide enough to accommodate a horse. Exhibiting lightning rapidity, striking before Pétion could utter a single sound, the snake snapped its mouth shut over its prey, then reared back.

Blade felt revulsion at the ghastly sight. He could see Pétion's ankles and feet jutting from between the reptile's lips, the black shoes kicking and twisting, and then the snake tilted its head upward, gulped, and swallowed.

Pétion's feet disappeared.

A bulge formed in the serpent's throat just behind the jaw. For over a minute the snake didn't move except for the rippling of its scaly skin as the bulge flowed down its throat. Pressure from within distended its neck as Pétion went into his death throes, thrashing and tossing wildly.

Blade almost stood and fired. He wanted to kill the serpent, but the realization that their weapons might not be adequate for the job deterred him. If he was going to take the reptile on, he would prefer to do it when he had an edge, some way of evening the odds.

At last the snake turned and headed to the southeast, its head held low to the water, moving swiftly.

The Warrior waited until the reptile was out of sight before standing. "Just when you think you've seen everything," he muttered.

"That thing scared Gremlin, yes?" the humanoid said, rising. He removed the sunglasses and tossed them aside.

Ferret stood and took several strides toward the bayou, his countenance registering severe agitation. "Did you see that sucker?" he asked absently.

"Who could miss it?" Blade quipped.

"What the hell are we doing here?" Ferret queried, gesturing at the water. "I mean, what the *hell* are we doing here?"

"You know the reason we came to New Orleans," Blade said. "To find the party responsible for the distress call and to help the people here in their fight against the Black Snake Society." His eyes enlarged in amazement as the obvious finally dawned on him. The Black Snake Society!

"No, you came to help some poor saps fight for their freedom," Ferret corrected him angrily. "Gremlin and I came because we're morons! Because we let Lynx sucker us in again!''

"It's no use crying over spilt milk, no?" Gremlin commented.

"I'm not worried about spilling milk, damn it," Ferret snapped. "I'm worried about spilling our blood. Didn't you see the size of that thing?"

"Of course, yes."

"And didn't it occur to you that we don't stand a prayer against a mutation as big as a mountain?"

"We'll find a way to destroy it, yes," Gremlin asserted optimistically.

"Yeah. Sure. Right. All we have to do is round up a mongoose forty feet long and we're in business."

Gremlin glanced at Blade. "Excuse him, yes? A few little problems and he tends to fall to pieces."

"Little!" Ferret bellowed. "If that snake gets any bigger, it'll start snacking on elephants."

"That's impossible, no?" Gremlin responded, and snickered. "There are no elephants in this region, yes?"

"You know what I mean," Ferret stated.

Blade hefted the Thompson and turned. "Enough chitchat. We've got to find Lynx." He bore to the northeast.

"Lynx," Ferret hissed. "This is all his fault. We've got weirdos who go around talking to giant snakes trying to blow us away, and the giant snakes they talk to ready to eat us if we show our faces." He paused. "I swear. If Lynx *ever* suggests we go on another mission, and I don't care if it's just to step outside the Home to gather blackberries, I'm going to belt him in the mouth."

"That's a good point," Blade said.

"What is?" Ferret asked in surprise.

"Is there just that one snake or dozens roaming these swamps?" Blade wondered.

"Dozens?" Ferret repeated, and glanced around nervously. "Nah. There couldn't be. Could there?"

"Maybe the Black Snake Society made the snake with

magic, yes?'' Gremlin theorized.

"Don't be crazy," Ferret said. "That voodoo stuff is a bunch of crap."

"You never know, no?"

"I know if you keep talking like this, I'm going to belt *you* in the mouth."

Gremlin glanced at his friend in dismay. "Ferret wouldn't hurt Gremlin, yes?"

"No. Of course not. It was just a figure of speech," Ferret replied uncomfortably. "I'd never hurt you."

"Good."

"But I could kill Lynx."

Blade smiled and stepped over a log. He planned to return to the vicinity of the cabin. If Lynx had been captured, then the cat-man should be in that area. If not, taking another of the *tonton macoutes* prisoner might enable them to learn critical information essential to the success of the operation. For starters, he'd like to know the identity of the leader of the Black Snake Society. Locating the voodoo sect's base of operations was equally important.

The minutes dragged by as the trio hiked onward. Overhead the afternoon sun arced steadily toward the west horizon.

"You know, I don't like the idea of being out here after dark," Ferret remarked. "I hope we find a safe place to stay for the night."

"We can always climb a tree, no?" Gremlin said.

"No," Ferret replied. "For all we know there could be humongous caterpillars crawling around up there."

The humanoid chuckled. "Ferret has a great sense of humor, yes?"

"I wish."

Blade abruptly halted and motioned for silence. He crouched, then moved ahead until he reached a cypress tree. Exercising supreme care, he peered around the trunk and spied the cabin approximately one hundred yards away.

Over two dozen members of the Black Snake Society were gathered around the structure.

Blade saw a powerfully built man in black addressing the other *tonton macoutes*. Was that the man Pétion had referred to, the man he'd called the Baron? Was the Baron even the head of the sect? He sensed, rather than heard, the hybrids join him.

"What's going on?" Ferret whispered.

"It looks like they've called off the hunt for us," Blade said softly.

"But why? One of their own is missing, no?" Gremlin mentioned.

Blade had no answer to that one. He watched as the magicians, as Pétion had called them, formed into a single file and marched to the east.

"They're leaving," Ferret exclaimed. "See? Even they don't want to be out here after dark."

"They could have a camp near here, yes?" Gremlin noted.

"Don't you get tired of looking at the bright side all the time?" Ferret asked.

"Shut your faces," Blade directed. He straightened, keeping his body flush with the trees, and thoughtfully observed the departure of the *tonton macoutes*. The notion of sending one of the hybrids to follow the men in black appealed to him, but after losing Lynx, and with night fast approaching, he didn't want to become separated from the other two. After the final man in line had vanished in the distance, he stepped into the open. "To the cabin."

"May I talk, no?" Gremlin inquired.

"Go ahead."

"Shouldn't one of us go to New Orleans, yes? You can go and Ferret and Gremlin will wait here for Lynx."

"The three of us will venture to New Orleans in the morning whether Lynx shows up or not," Blade informed them.

"I thought Warriors never abandon other Warriors,"

Ferret said.

"They don't," Blade agreed. "But has it ever occurred to you that Lynx might be in their hands and already on his way to the city?"

"But what if he's not, no?" Gremlin asked, sounding worried. "How will Lynx know where to find us, yes?"

"If he doesn't show up, we'll leave him a note. I have paper in my backpack," Blade said.

The rest of the distance to the cabin was covered in silence. As before, the cabin door stood wide open.

Blade made for the entrance. Perhaps—just perhaps—the *tonton macoutes* had left a clue behind that would prove helpful. The possibility was remote, but he had to check. He advanced to the doorway, then looked back. "Keep your eyes peeled. Stay alert."

"I'm always alert when there's the chance I might be jumped by a man-eating snake or caterpillar," Ferret cracked.

Blade grinned and lifted his right leg to go inside.

That was when the burly form in black materialized in front of him and jammed a submachine gun barrel into his ribs.

CHAPTER
TEN

The wild boar rushed toward them like a great, hairy battering ram.

There was no time to flee and nowhere to run if they could. Without an avenue of escape, Lynx had a single option: to fight. Which suited him just fine. He was tired of running anyway.

Eleanore screamed.

Lynx shoved her to the ground and shouted, "Don't move!" Then he skipped to the left a foot, causing the boar to angle at him and ignore the woman. He had barely braced himself for the onslaught when the beast was on him.

The boar's tusks stabbed at the hybrid's chest.

Lynx dodged to the left, but his delayed reaction cost him dearly. The tusks clipped his torso, gouging a slim furrow in his ribs, and the impact sent him sailing ten feet to crash onto his back in the weeds.

Displaying remarkable agility, the wild boar stopped, wheeled, and charged once more.

Furious at being struck and aggravated by the pain, Lynx pushed to his feet and tensed his legs. Not this time, sucker!

he thought, and curled his fingers into claws. A peculiar
trilling sound issued from his lips, a sound he made when
either perplexed or enraged. At the moment he wasn't
perplexed.

The boar's hoofs were drumming on the earth, and it was
grunting its displeasure at having intruders invade its domain,
its elemental savagery dictating that it tear, rend, destroy.
With its ears flattened and its typically uncoiled tail straight
out, the living tank homed in for the kill.

This time Lynx was prepared. He waited until the boar
had closed to within a yard, then leaped high into the air,
his feline sinews carrying him clear over the boar's head and
shoulders. In midair he twisted and came down, landing on
the beast's back. Instantly he tore into the swine, ripping and
slashing with sharp nails that resembled genuine claws but
weren't retractable. The boar's tough hide resisted his first
few swipes, but in a moment he penetrated to the softer flesh
underneath and really went to work.

Eleanore DeCoud witnessed the battle in stupefied
bewilderment. Lying propped on her elbows, she was too
astonished to move. When the boar initially sprang at them,
she'd expected to die. No one, not even someone endowed
with Lynx's obviously superior strength, could hope to best
a wild boar in one-on-one combat. Or so she believed.

But the hybrid was doing his best to prove her wrong.

Lynx bared his pointed teeth, reveling in the opportunity
to give his animal nature free rein, and buried his nails several
inches in the boar's muscular tissue.

The beast ran in a zigzag pattern, whipping its body from
side to side, striving to dislodge the bantam hybrid causing
it such torment. Sensing that its tactics were of no avail, the
boar instinctively decided to try a maneuver that worked for
removing troublesome burrs from its coat and alleviating a
bothersome itch. It ran straight for the forest and the nearest
tree.

Absorbed in slicing and dicing the swine's back, Lynx
didn't realize the new danger until he dimly realized that

someone was yelling his name. He glanced up, startled to behold an oak tree not six feet away, and he began to vault to safety.

Too late.

A low-hanging limb appeared out of nowhere and caught Lynx in the chest, knocking the breath from his lungs and lifting him from the wild boar. He fell, stunned, and felt his left side strike the earth. In the recesses of his mind his own consciousness shrieked at him to get up, to get out of the way, because at any second the boar would come back for round two.

It did.

Lynx heard the hoofbeats first and swung his head to the west. The beast was streaking toward him, its beady eyes radiating hatred, its back and sides coated with a spreading crimson stain. Lynx rolled frantically to the north, and it seemed as if an earthquake rattled the ground as the boar thundered past.

Get up!

Inhaling raggedly, his chest in exquisite agony, Lynx stood and staggered, feeling woozy, disoriented, and he shook his head to clear the mental cobwebs.

The wild boar was already racing toward him again.

Lynx backed up, stumbling, almost going down, until he bumped into something hard. His eyes on the beast, he reached behind him and brushed his palm against the trunk of the oak.

The tree!

A crazy idea blossomed in his pain-racked brain, a means of turning the tables on his incensed adversary if only he could muster the strength.

The boar was 20 feet away, its driving hoofs throwing up clods of dirt, its head lowered in anticipation of goring the feline with its tusks.

Come and get me! Lynx thought, and focused on the beast's snout. Timing would be everything. If he misjudged the distance, if he miscalculated by a hairsbreadth, he was as good as dead. Those tusks would disembowel him as easily as one of Blade's bowies could carve up a melon.

Only ten feet separated the hybrid and the boar.

"Lynx! Look out!" Eleanore DeCoud shouted.

What? Did she think he didn't see it? Lynx would have laughed, but there was no time left for anything except putting his plan into effect. He took a deep breath, waited until the absolutely last instant, waited until those pointed tusks were spearing toward his midsection, and sprang straight up, leaping for a branch close at hand.

The boar couldn't stop.

Lynx looked down and saw the beast's head slam into the trunk with titanic force. The entire tree swayed, and the branch he clasped bobbed as if in a strong wind.

Stunned, the boar slumped, its front legs buckling.

"My turn!" Lynx hissed, and let go of the limb. He dropped onto the boar, angling his fall to land astride the animal's front shoulders, and before the boar could rise he bent forward and sank his nails into the swine's neck.

The boar squealed and struggled to stand.

A frenzy seized Lynx, an uncontrollable impulse to rend and rip, and rend and rip he did, concentrating his energy on the boar's throat, slashing flesh and severing veins and arteries, his hands a blur, his arms coated with crimson and gore up to the elbows.

Blood gushed from the beast's neck in red torrents, spraying the grass and soaking the ground. The boar thrashed and tried once again to regain its footing, but it slipped in its own life fluid and fell.

Lynx kept tearing at his foe. Both sides of the beast's neck were thin ribbons. He tore a chunk of tissue free and drove his nails even deeper.

The boar's movements became weaker and weaker. It sluggishly lifted its head and thrashed, grunting feebly.

Die! Die! Die! Lynx screamed in his mind. He was winning and he wasn't about to stop for anything. His nails tore and shredded tirelessly. The boar's head lay on the earth, yet he had no intention of stopping. His shoulders began to ache, but he continued. Cutting, always cutting, until a hand touched his shoulder and a voice spoke gently in his ear.

"Lynx! You can stop! The thing is dead!"

Dead? The word registered through the scarlet haze enveloping Lynx's consciousness and he paused, breathing deeply. "What?" he blurted out, the word seeming to echo hollowly as if spoken by someone else at a great distance.

"The boar is dead," Eleanor repeated.

Lynx blinked and stared at the ravaged carcass underneath him, at the strips of dangling flesh and the exposed spine. "Oh."

"Are you okay?"

"Fine," Lynx mumbled. "Just peachy." He slid from the swine and straightened slowly. His chest felt like he'd just been run over by a military convoy truck.

"Are you sure?"

"Quit naggin' me, woman," Lynx said. He shuffled to the north and sat down on a log, suddenly overcome with a pervading weariness, his arms and legs leaden.

"I just asked," Eleanore stated testily.

"I didn't mean to hurt your feelings," Lynx told her. He touched his chest where the branch had struck him and flinched.

Eleanore came right over. "Are any bones broken?"

"Don't think so," Lynx replied. "Just hurts like hell." He looked up at her, surprised at the genuine concern reflected on her features, and felt a shade guilty at the gruff treatment he'd dispensed since capturing her.

"You were magnificent. I've never seen anyone do what you did."

"I didn't have much choice," Lynx reminded her. "It was either Ugly or me. And my wife would be ticked off if I went and got myself killed by an overgrown pig."

"Can I get you something? Do you need some water?" Eleanore inquired.

Lynx almost said yes. He was terribly thirsty. But he

envisioned her going near the swamp and being jumped by one of those big gators. "No," he answered hoarsely. "I'm fine."

"I don't mind getting some."

"No," Lynx reiterated sternly, then softened when he saw her frown. "Thanks anyway."

"Anytime."

Lynx placed his hands on the rough log and leaned back to study her intently. "You know, I guess I was wrong about you."

"How so?"

"I think I can trust you."

Eleanore smiled. "Thank you. I'm really not one of the bad guys."

"Then you'd better figure out who is."

"What?"

"Who else knows about the shortwave radio and the cabin?"

"Only a few people," Eleanore said, her forehead creased, contemplating the significance of his remarks. "Surely you're not suggesting that someone in the Resistance is a traitor?"

"I'm not suggesting nothin'. I'm flat out tellin' you that you've got a snitch in your organization."

"Impossible."

"Then how'd those voodoo bozos know where to find you?"

Eleanore's lips compressed. She had no answer for that one.

"Think about it," Lynx advised, and looked down at the tissue, hair, and blood caking his arms. "What a mess. They sure don't make wild boars like they used to."

"You've done that before, haven't you?"

"Nope. I've never tangled with a boar before."

"That's not what I meant and you know it," Eleanore stated. "You've torn things apart with your bare hands before.."

"Once or twice." Lynx gazed at her. "Why?"

"I figured as much."

"Why? Because I threatened to rip your throat apart earlier?"

"No. Because of the look on your face as you were fighting the boar."

"What about it?"

Eleanore's voice lowered when she answered. "You looked as if you were enjoying yourself. I mean *thoroughly* enjoying yourself. Am I right?"

"It was the most fun I've had in ages."

"You call nearly being gored fun?"

Lynx shrugged, then grimaced at the discomfort the simple motion caused. "Beats playin' a dull game of checkers."

"I'll never understand you."

"There's not a whole lot to understand. I was created in a laboratory by a madman who brought me into existence for one reason and one reason only."

"Which was?"

"To kill."

"Oh."

An uncomfortable silence descended for all of ten seconds.

"Well, we'd best get our butts in gear," Lynx proposed, and stood.

"Are you certain you're up to it? You took quite a beating," Eleanore said.

"I'm no wimp, lady. A little tussle like that hardly fazes me."

"Then why are you gritting your teeth and holding your side?"

"Constipation," Lynx declared.

"I vote we rest until you've recovered."

"This ain't no democracy."

"Okay. Then how's this for a reason, smart guy," Eleanore snapped. "Wild boars don't usually travel alone."

"They don't?"

"No, genius. Even the males will band together in small groups for mutual protection."

Lynx scanned the forest, probing the shadows. "Then there could be more around."

"Your wife must have married you for your intellect," Eleanore cracked.

"Okay. Don't get personal. We'll rest for a while," Lynx stated. "Fifteen minutes, maximum."

"Whatever you say."

Lynx sat back down, relieved at the opportunity to rest. Truth to tell, he felt like crap. A few minutes of recuperation would do him a world of good. He glanced up at Eleanore and saw her gazing in fearful astonishment over his head at something to the north. Another wild boar! Lynx deduced, and twisted.

Only it wasn't another boar.

Thirty feet away, a rifle pressed to his right shoulder, stood one of the men in black.

CHAPTER
ELEVEN

"If you so much as twitch, *monsieur*, you are dead," the burly man stated.

Blade froze. Even his lightning reflexes wouldn't enable him to evade a bullet at point-blank range. He defiantly returned the hostile stare of the *tonton macoute*, his right leg suspended in midair. Ferret and Gremlin apparently tried to bring their weapons into play, because the burly man in black barked a warning.

"Try anything and your big friend is fish bait! *Comprenez-vous?* Do you understand?"

A few tense moments went by.

"Yeah, we understand, scumsucker," Ferret snapped.

"Then you will lower your assault rifles to the ground and raise your hands."

Blade heard the dull clatter as the pair of AR-15's fell to the turf.

"You are sensible . . . things," the man said, smirking. He puckered his thick lips and vented a piercing whistle.

"Calling the other dogs?" Blade baited him.

"Your insults are wasted on me, *monsieur*. Save your

breath," the man stated, and repeated the whistle.

Footsteps sounded, coming around both sides of the cabin.

Out of the corners of his eyes Blade glimpsed more members of the voodoo sect coming to their companion's aid. He chided himself for being the champion idiot of the Western Hemisphere. How could he have blundered into their trap so easily? He must be slipping.

"I'll be damned!" a newcomer declared. "Now I owe that strutting peacock François an apology. His plan worked."

Blade tensed when hands and arms came into view and disarmed him, taking the Thompson and both Bowies. His backpack was also removed.

Once all the giant's weapons were taken, the man in the doorway grinned. "You can set your leg down now and step back."

Frowning at his stupidity, Blade moved rearward a few feet and turned.

Six *tonton macoutes* had their guns trained on the hybrids. One of the men in black had the Thompson over a shoulder. Another man, the one nearest to Blade, the one with the Bowies tucked under his belt, the same one who had made the comment about the peacock, grinned at the Warrior.

"Hey, man. Do you have any idea how embarrassed I will be?"

Blade said nothing. He noticed the cult member spoke with an unusual accent. The word "man" came out as "mon."

"That François will never let me hear the end of it," the guy said.

Still Blade kept silent.

"What's the matter? Cat got your tongue, man?" The talkative fellow studied the giant for a bit, then smiled. "Oh, Maybe I should introduce myself. My friends all call me Jacques."

"Do you mind if I refer to you as Airhead?" Blade finally spoke up.

"Whoa! A hardass. I like that," Jacques said, and laughed. "You should be fun at the ceremony."

"What ceremony?"

Jacques leaned toward the Warrior and smirked. "That's for me to know, man, and for you to find out about the hard way."

"I can hardly wait."

"Let's quit playing around with this bastard and take off," the burly man in the doorway suggested. "If we hurry we can catch François."

"Can't wait to get your nose brown, eh?" Jacques said.

The burly man emerged from the cabin. "Don't talk to me like that."

"Why not? Everybody knows François and you are best buddies," Jacques stated, stressing the last two words sarcastically.

"I warn you—" the burly man began.

Jacques swung the Uzi he held in a short arc and pointed the barrel at the other man. "Don't threaten me, Pierre. Don't ever threaten me. I'm the sergeant here, not you. And I say we will catch the good captain when we catch him. *Comprenez-vous*?"

Pierre's lips twitched but he made no move to employ his weapon. "*Je comprends.*"

"Good," Jacques growled, and slowly lowered the Uzi. "Now you will be so kind as to tie our prisoners so we can get going."

Blade had observed the confrontation with interest. Friction in an enemy camp could sometimes be turned to an advantage. He frowned as Pierre stepped up to him. "What if I give my word to be a good little boy?"

"Please, man," Jacques said. "Don't be insulting my intelligence. You'll try to escape the first chance you get."

The Warrior shrugged. "It never hurts to try."

Pierre pulled a black nylon cord from his right front pocket. "Hold out your hands," he snapped.

Reluctantly, well aware of the guns leveled in his direction, Blade complied. In a minute his wrists were securely bound.

"There," Pierre said, and stepped back. "That should hold

you." He moved over to Ferret.

Blade looked at the man called Jacques. "Did I hear correctly? Are you a sergeant?"

"I sure am."

"Then the *tonton macoutes* is a military organization? I was told that you considered yourselves magicians."

"And where did you hear that bit of news, man?"

"From someone you probably know. Henri Pétion."

The mention of the dead man's name caused all of the men in black to glance at the giant.

"Henri is missing," Jacques stated. "You wouldn't happen to know where he is?"

"As a matter of fact I do. He should be halfway digested by now," Blade disclosed.

Jacques's bafflement showed. "Pardon?"

"Henri is history. He was swallowed by a huge snake," Blade told them, and was immediately surprised by their reactions. Every man appeared stunned and they exchanged startled glances.

"What do you mean, man?" Jacques asked harshly.

"Just what I said. Pétion was eaten by an enormous black snake about forty feet long. He let the thing come right up to him. Even talked to it. Talk about nut cases."

Jacques swallowed and moved closer to the Warrior. "Did he call this snake by name?"

"Yeah. He kept calling it Damballah."

"Liar!" Pierre suddenly exploded. He aimed his submachine gun at the giant's chest. "You rotten liar! You'll die for your blasphemy!"

"No!" Jacques cried out, and stepped between them. "Don't shoot him."

"You heard the lie he just told about Damballah!" Pierre declalred. "He deserves to die on the spot."

"That decision isn't up to us. Only the Baron can determine this man's fate."

Slowly, demonstrating a marked disinclination, Pierre lowered his weapon and fixed his mirrored sunglasses on the strapping prisoner. "I hope the Baron will give you to me. I'll make you pay for mouthing such foul fabrications."

"The truth hurts, huh?" Blade cracked.

"Enough of this," Jacques barked. He nodded at the hybrids. "Finish tying these creatures and we can get the hell out of here. We must inform the Baron about Henri."

"You don't believe this bastard, do you?" Pierre queried.

Jacques studied the giant critically for a moment. "I don't know what to believe. But I do know we must report to the Baron right away. So get the furry one and the gray one tied, *s'il vous plaît.*"

"Right away," Pierre said, and moved to obey.

"What's all the fuss over a reptilian mutation?" Blade casually inquired.

"Damballah is no mere mutation, man," Jacques replied. "Damballah is our God."

"You worship a mutant?"

"Didn't you hear me? Damballah is the Snake God, the living source of our power. Others may worship mere symbols. We worship our god in the flesh."

"How fitting."

"What do you mean?"

"You think you're worshipping your god in the flesh, yet this so-called god will eat your flesh in one gulp if you give it half a chance."

Thoughtful lines etched Jacques's features. "If it's true what you say, if Damballah truly did eat Henri, then Henri must have done something to displease our great lord."

"The only mistake Henri made was forgetting the basic rule of dealing with animals."

"Which rule is this?"

"Never trust an animal that can eat you for din-din."

Jacques actually grinned. "You have a sense of humor, Monsieur. *Je l'aime beaucoup.*"

"You speak French fluently," Blade noted.

"A little French, a little Spanish. Mostly I speak English. And Creole, of course."

"Never heard of it."

"Then you are not from New Orleans or anywhere within a hundred miles of the city. Everyone in these parts knows about Creole. It's a French dialect, but it includes many Spanish, Indian, and English words," Jacques related, and cocked his head to one side. "So where are you from, big one?"

"That's for me to know and you to wish you did."

"Will you at least tell me your name?"

"Dieneces."

"A very unusual name, man."

"Not to Herodotus."

"Who?"

"Never mind," Blade said, suppressing a smile.

Jacques turned toward the hybrids. "And what are the names of these most unusual creatures?"

"Why don't you ask them."

"Very well, man. I will." Jacques stepped over to Ferret and Gremlin, who stood side by side with their wrists tied. "Who are you?"

"I often wonder the same thing," Ferret replied.

"Sorry, but that's secret information, yes?" Gremlin said.

Mildly exasperated, Jacques placed his left hand on his hip and hefted the Uzi. "You won't tell me?"

Ferret looked at Gremlin. "He's pretty sharp for a moron."

"Must be a fluke, no?"

"That's enough out of you. Neither of you will speak unless spoken to," Jacques declared.

"Fine by me, camel-breath," Ferret retorted.

In one stride Jacques was standing directly in front of the feisty hybrid. He brutally rammed the Uzi barrel into Ferret's stomach, doubling the mutant over, and then slammed the submachine gun against Ferret's temple.

Stagered by the blow, the hybrid dropped to his knees.

"I'll teach you to badmouth me, man," Jacques said, and raised the Uzi to deliver another strike. Only it never landed.

A pair of steely arms unexpectedly looped over his head and constricted around his neck, instantaneously cutting off his air, choking him with frightful rapidity. He started to struggle and a flinty voice spoke in his right ear.

"My wrists may be tied, but I can still break your neck like a twig if you hit him again. Tell your buddies to lower their weapons."

Jacques glanced to the right and the left, and saw his companions had swung their weapons to cover the giant. If they fired at such close range, they would inevitably also hit him. The pressure on his neck slacked off slightly and he blurted out, "Don't shoot!"

"I can nail him in the back," Pierre said from somewhere to the rear.

"No, you fool! The bullets will pass completely through him and hit me!" Jacques cried. "Don't fire!"

"Tell them to lower their weapons," Blade repeated.

Jacques took a deep breath and responded boldly. "No."

"No?"

"They won't lower their guns, man. Look, I know you can kill me if you want. But what would it gain you? My men would mow you down where you stand. Why not be reasonable? Release me, and I give you my word I will not hit your furry friend again. What do you say?"

Blade had no other option. The *tonton macoutes* held the upper hand for the moment. He was surrounded and outgunned. Besides, he had accomplished his purpose in saving Ferret from a further beating. "All right," he said, and lifted his arms over the sergeant's head, then took a pace backwards.

Jacques spun, rubbing his sore throat, and appraised the giant with a mixture of anger and fear. He stared at the prisoner's bulging biceps and triceps respectfully, knowing full well he could easily have been killed. "Okay," he stated, a bit hoarsely. "Move out. Pierre, take the point. The three prisoners will be in the middle."

Gremlin helped Ferret to stand.

"And not a peep out of any of you," Jacques warned the trio.

Blade moved closer to his friends, and in seconds they were underway, tramping eastward, hemmed in by their enemies. He smiled reassuringly at Ferret when the hybrid glanced back appreciatively. Holding his arms next to his body, he began working at the nylon cord, surreptitiously flexing his arms as far apart as they would go, relaxing, and repeating the action. Sooner or later he would loosen the cord sufficiently so he could slip his hands free.

Then the *tonton macoutes* had better watch out.

There would be hell to pay.

CHAPTER TWELVE

"Stay where you are!" the man in black called out.

Lynx's mind raced. Where there was one scuzzbucket, there were probably more. If he didn't do something—anything—and do it fast, the woman and he were as good as caught. The SOB was too far away to take out, which meant resorting to evasive action. "No problem!" he shouted, and stood, blocking the man's view of Eleanore.

"Step aside!" the scuzzbucket ordered.

"Okay," Lynx replied cheerily, and went into action, whirling and driving his right shoulder into the woman, bearing both of them to the ground.

The rifle boomed and a slug thudded into the log.

"Stay close," Lynx said, and crawled quickly to his right, toward the oak tree. Once there, he rose into a squat and peeked past the trunk.

The man in black was running for the log.

Snickering, Lynx darted into the undergrowth, pausing just long enough for Eleanore to reach his side. He angled into the densest thicket he could find, squeezing in until he came to an open spot, ignoring the jabs of the short, thin branches.

Eleanore eased next to him. "What now?" she whispered.

"Shhhhh," Lynx cautioned, listening.

Loud voices penetrated the brush.

"What happened?"

"I saw two of them. A hairy thing and DeCoud. They got away."

"Fool! Did you hit them?"

"I don't think so, Captain François."

"What is that?"

"What?"

"No wonder you missed. You can't even see a dead boar lying ten feet in front of you."

"*Mon Dieu!*"

"Simpleton."

Five seconds of quiet ensued.

"The hairy one must have done this to the boar. *Trés formidable,* no?"

"Nothing human could do this, Captain."

"Figured that out all by yourself, did you? Come. We must get to the boats. The Baron will be waiting for us."

"But the hairy creature and the girl?"

"They are trapped here without a means of navigating the bayou. In a few days we will return and find their putrid corpses. Right now we have the ceremony to consider. Midnight will be here before we know it."

"I can hardly wait, Captain. Damballah will be very pleased."

The voices began to fade as the speakers bore to the north.

"The Baron and Majesta have promised something special for tonight."

"Did they say—"

"—multiple sacrifices, which will—"

"—Snake God—"

Lynx strained to hear additional details, but the pair of *tonton macoutes* were too far off.

"Did they mention multiple sacrifices?" Eleanore queried.

"I could barely make out the words."

"Yeah."

"Dear God! They must mean Jerry and Adrien. We've got to save them."

"How? There are dozens of them and only two of us."

"We can go into New Orleans. Violet will know what to do."

"Who?"

"Violet is the leader of the Resistance. She's also an old friend of mine. We go back a long way."

Lynx flattened and squirmed out of the thicket. "I'm not leavin' until I locate my buddies." He stood and waited for her to join him.

"For all you know they could be dead or captured," Eleanore noted as she rose and ran her fingers through her hair. "It makes more sense to head for New Orleans."

"Feminine logic never ceases to amaze me," Lynx declared, and grabbed her by the right wrist. "Come on." He marched northward, pulling her along.

"What's this? I thought we were friends?"

"We are. If we weren't, I'd slug you and throw you over my shoulder."

"Please, Lynx. Let go."

"Just move your tush and quit yakkin'."

"I can't keep going."

"Sure you can. It's easy. Just keep puttin' one foot in front of the other."

"You don't understand," Eleanore said weakly, and unexpectedly collapsed, falling to her knees.

Lynx turned, his expression contorted in anger until he saw her eyelids fluttering and realized she was about to pitch onto her face. He stooped and caught her in his arms. "What's wrong with you?"

Eleanore mustered a wan smile. "Haven't eaten for almost two days, remember?" She sagged in his arms, her eyes closing.

"Damn," Lynx growled. *Now* what should he do? She needed food, but he wanted to search for Ferret, Gremlin,

and Blade. In her weakened state she was bound to slow him
down. Either he fed her or carried her. He looked back at
the dead boar and contemplated tearing out a large chunk
of fresh meat. A steak would undoubtedly revive her.
Unfortunately, he doubted she would eat the meat raw like
he often did, which meant taking the time to get a fire going
and roasting the flesh. Since he didn't have matches, starting
a fire would be a bitch.

Double damn.

Lynx decided to compromise. He scooped her unconscious
form into his arms and jogged to the north. He'd carry her
until they came across something edible or his pals,
whichever he found first. So resolved, he moved at a swift
clip, the pain in his chest having subsided to a tolerable level.
His wiry form flowed over the ground with the athletic grace
of his namesake, and his nostrils constantly quivered as he
tested the air for scent.

He thought of his mate, Melody, and experienced a twinge
of guilt at leaving her alone to traipse off to Louisiana. She
had hugged him with tears moistening her lovely eyes just
before he stepped out the door and urged him to be careful.
Not that he would ever be otherwise.

Caution was his middle name.

Well, sort of.

Lynx pondered on what his next move should be if he
failed to hook up with his companions. For the first time
the idea that he might wind up stranded in New Orleans
occurred to him, and his brow knit in intense contemplation.
Talk about gonad-busters. If he wound up stranded, he'd have
to fight his way across hundreds of miles of hostile countryside to reach the Home, probably taking on countless
scavengers and mutations in the process. A grin creased his
thin lips.

Bop his way over hundreds of miles, huh?

Maybe being stranded had its plus side too.

The prospect of going against so many adversaries, instead
of filling him with dread or at the least a sense of realistic

reservation, actually appealed to his genetically created capacity for action and mayhem. He loved a good fight almost as much as he did anything—maybe even more—and he anticipated such a hazardous journey with relish.

Bring on the wimps!

He'd waste every one.

Lynx glanced at the sun hovering in the western sky, acutely conscious of the dwindling daylight hours, and increased his speed. If he didn't locate the others, he at least wanted to find a safe place to spend the night. Not for his sake so much as for the woman. In her frail condition another night exposed to the elements could precipatate an illness.

That, and the fact a lot of gators and snakes were nocturnal; they did most of their hunting in the cool of the night.

He definitely didn't want to bump into a snake in the dark. Even little snakes gave him the creeps, and had for as long as he could remember. Why, he had no idea.

For long minutes Lynx continued on his course, and he was about to stop and take a break so he could hunt for food for Eleanore, when from a couple of dozen yards ahead arose the sounds of voices. He was moving through an open stretch of field where the weeds reached past his waist. Ten feet to his left a solitary bush reared over six feet in height. He hunched over, holding the woman close to his chest, and darted to the bush.

The voices grew louder, indicating whoever was doing the talking must be approaching his position.

Lynx gently deposited Eleanore at the base of the bush and eased to the right until he could peer at the field beyond. He discovered he'd been mistaken; the voices weren't arising directly ahead, they were coming from a point 50 feet to the northwest.

A party of *tonton macoutes* was hiking from west to east along the faint trail.

Lynx vented his low trilling noise at the sight of the three figures in the middle of the file. Blade, Ferret, and Gremlin! Naturally, the dummies had been captured. He watched the group draw closer, thankful the bush must have partially screened him from their view.

None of the men in black were paying much attention to the terrain around them. They all appeared to be in a hurry and were walking briskly.

What was the big rush? Lynx wondered, and then recalled Captain François and the other dimwit. Those two must have been with another bunch of twits who passed by previously. Perhaps one of them had heard Eleanore's screams or shouts and the guy armed with the rifle had been sent to investigate.

Now this second group was trying to catch up with the first.

Pleased at his deductive insights, Lynx smirked and stayed motionless as the group passed to the east. He saw Ferret and Gremlin looking glum as all get-out, which certainly figured for two guys who possessed such negative attitudes about going on runs, and noticed Blade working secretly on the rope binding those stout wrists.

Leave it to the giant to be doing something instead of feeling sorry for himself.

Lynx waited until the party was almost out of sight, then lifted Eleanore again and raced in pursuit. He angled to the trail and took a right, keeping his body as low as he could. Unless the *tonton macoutes* halted and focused binoculars on their back trail, he seriously doubted they would spot him.

Eleanore groaned but did not regain consciousness.

Par for the course.

More minutes went by. Lynx could feel his leg muscles aching. He suppressed the discomfort and concentrated on the task at hand. His ability to focus his single-minded attention on one thing at a time had been unique even among the hybrids comprising the Genetic Research Division. When he had a job to do, he pursued his objective with an almost fanatical determination until the goal was achieved. Which partly explained why he had been pushing, pushing, pushing to go on a mission with the Big Guy.

His personal philosophy on life had always been short and simple. When you want something, go after it with gusto.

When obstacles get in your way, crush them. Go with the gut and live life to the max.

What else mattered?

Until he met the Family, he would have said, "Nothing." But after knowing those do-gooders for so many years, after witnessing the life-style they led, after seeing their devotion to higher spiritual ideals most people regarded as old-fashioned or downright wacko, now he wasn't so certain.

Maybe there was something to that Supreme Source jazz after all.

If heavy hitters like Blade, Yama, Rikki, and Samson believed in all that stuff, then it might be worth looking into someday. What was that favorite expression of the Elders? Oh, yeah. Every person should grow his or her own spiritual experience. And the practice clearly worked as far as the Family members were concerned.

Blade, Yama, Rikki, and Samson all believed in that spirit stuff, but each one in a different way. Rikki was into the martial arts, into becoming the perfected spiritual sword-master, whatever the hell that meant. Yama seemed intent on becoming as proficient in dispensing death as the Hindu King of Death whose name he had adopted. And Samson—well, Samson was one of those yokels who believed every word of the Bible was inviolate. Samson's faith was as solid as the proverbial rock. And although Lynx liked to tease him about his unshakable devotion, secretly Lynx was tremendously impressed by such sterling loyalty.

The head Warrior occupied a class all his own. Blade seldom talked about his profound religious beliefs, yet anyone who knew him for any length of time knew the giant possessed faith as unshakable as Samson's, as devoted to perfection as Rikki's, but a faith that didn't prevent him from being even more lethal than Yama.

Go figure.

The scent of water brought an end to Lynx's reflection, and he gazed to the east and spied a body of shallow water, more swamp stretching to the east. And he heard more voices conversing.

Cautious now, he slowed and crept carefully forward, his head barely above the weeds. In 15 yards he could hear the conversation and he halted.

"—off about five minutes ago."

"Damn it! I knew we should have hurried faster."

"Shut your lip, Pierre. We'll take these boats and be back at the estate in two hours."

"What about us?" a man asked anxiously.

"What about you?" someone responded in an authoritative tone.

"Captain François told us to stay put until everyone has been accounted for. He took the bodies of our brothers who were killed by these bastards with him. And now you show up, Jacques, with everyone else except Pétion. Do you happen to know where he is?"

"Dead, according to the one with all the muscles."

"How did Henri die?"

There was an extended pause.

"These three claim Damballah ate him," the man named Jacques replied.

Lynx heard the men uttering oaths in a foreign tongue. Then one of them, the one who had been doing most of the talking, spoke again.

"They lie!"

"Pierre feels the same way."

"Don't *you*?"

"I doubt they speak the truth, but I honestly don't know," Jacques stated.

"Perhaps, to play it safe, we should stay here until nightfall," suggested the other one of the pair who had cursed vehemently. "Since these sons of bitches are undoubtedly lying, Henri might yet show up."

Lynx pursed his lips. What was this business about some guy named Henri? Had the bozo really been eaten by that giant snake Eleanore had mentioned? He was about to inch closer when he felt a rubbing sensation on his feet, and he looked down to behold an olive, stout-bodied snake with a broad-based, flat-topped head distinguished by distinct holes on each side between the eye and the nostril, the traditional trademark of a pit viper.

CHAPTER THIRTEEN

"Suit yourselves," Jacques said to the two men who had been assigned to stay by the boats. "You are probably right to stay. The Baron would be extremely displeased if we abandoned one of our own without probable cause." He turned and motioned at one of the boats. "Get in, Dieneces."

For a few seconds Blade stood there at the water's edge, preoccupied with thoughts of escaping, and completely forgetting the name he had given the sergeant.

"Didn't you hear me?" Jacques demanded. "Get in the damn boat, man."

The giant glanced at the man in black, then entered the nearest of the four unusual boats in front of him. The craft were about twelve feet long, with low sides and a shallow displacement, ideal for navigating marshy terrain. Each one could accommodate six people easily. Every boat sported an outboard motor.

"Sit in the middle," Jacques directed.

Blade eased down on the center thwart and placed his wrists between his legs.

Ferret and Gremlin moved toward the same boat.

"Not you two!" Jacques snapped. "Only one of you to a boat. That way there is less chance of you giving us trouble."

Demonstrating obvious reluctance, the hybrids parted and stepped onto different crafts.

The sergeant issued brisk instructions to his men, and a pair of *tonton macoutes* climbed on each boat with the hybrids, one man sitting in the front with his weapon trained on each captive while the second man handled the outboard.

Blade scowled when three of the men in black came on the craft he occupied. Jacques took the seat at the front, smirking triumphantly as he sat down. The two others sat behind the Warrior, next to the motor.

"You don't look very happy, *mon ami*," the sergeant commented.

"It's all this air pollution."

"Beg pardon?"

"When was the last time you took a bath?"

Jacques, surprisingly, chuckled. "Definitely a fine sense of humor. What a waste." He glanced at the man seated at the stern. "Get underway. The other boats will follow us."

Blade listened in resignation as the outboards were started and revved. He stared eastward as the lines were hauled in and the three boats headed across the bayou.

"We have a long trip ahead of us," Jacques mentioned. "Feel free to talk if you want." He removed his sunglasses.

"Why are you being so kind?"

"A condemned man should not be made to suffer during his final hours on this world."

"I'm condemned, am I?"

"Not yet. But you will be tonight at the ceremony. The Baron will consign you to the sacrificial altar."

"What if I don't want to go?"

"I'm afraid you won't have much choice in the matter. The ceremony must be held so that our magic remains strong and effective."

"What kind of magic are we talking about here? The sort

where you pull a rabbit out of a hat?"

Jacques snorted. "The Black Snake Society doesn't indulge in child's pranks, man. We practice black magic, the only real magic. With it we control our destiny. We can make others do our bidding. When we call on the spirits, they do as we wish. Black magic is power, man. True power."

"And we all know absolute power corrupts absolutely."

"What?"

"Never mind," Blade said, and gazed out over the bayou. "Where exactly are we headed?"

"To Baron Laveau's estate."

"In New Orleans?"

"No. North of the city in the swamp," Jacques said, then added for emphasis, "far back in the swamp."

"How long have you been a member of the Society?" Blade casually inquired, while between his legs he strained against the nylon cord without being obvious about his effort.

"Six years."

"You must like it."

Jacques studied the giant, his brow furrowed. "Why all these questions, man? What do you care?"

"Humor me. I'm slated to die, remember?"

"Fair enough. I respect a man who has courage, and I think you are a man who has a lot," Jacques stated. "And yes, I like being in the Society. What else is there? If I wasn't one of the *tonton macoutes*, I'd be a nobody in New Orleans, one of the faceless masses living from day to day, hand to mouth, with no hope for a future."

"You sound as if you've given the matter a great deal of thought."

"Of course I have. Joining the Society is not an act a person does on the spur of the moment, not when taking the vow means you are bound to the Society for life."

"What vow?"

"The oath of allegiance to the Black Snake Society. The promise to serve Damballah for all your days. If a member breaks their oath, they are hunted down and taken back to the Baron." Jacques stopped and seemed to shudder. "You can't imagine the fate they endure."

"Pretty horrible, huh?"

"Horrible isn't the word, man! Traitors are skinned alive, then hung by their heels over a pit of alligators and slowly lowered down, an inch at a time. I've seen three men die in such a manner." Jacques closed his eyes for a moment. "Their screams will haunt me forever."

"I get the impression you'd quit the Society if you could."

Startled by the statement, Jacques glanced at the two men behind the giant, then glared at the Warrior. "No way, man! Where did you ever get a crazy idea like that? The Black Snake Society is my life. I serve the Baron and Majesta willingly and happily."

"Of course you do," Blade stated, amused by the fleeting panic in the man's eyes.

"Don't be talking like that, man."

"I won't do it again," Blade promised. His arms ached from the sustained strain and he felt either sweat or blood trickling down his hands.

"Jerk," Jacques snapped.

In order to continue distracting his captor, Blade kept the conversation going. "You never did answer me earlier."

"About what?"

"Your rank as a sergeant. And you mentioned a captain too. The *tonton macoutes* must be a quasi-military organization."

"There needs to be someone in charge, no?"

"You must be good at your job if you've been appointed a sergeant."

Jacques squared his shoulders. "I've never let the Baron down."

The cord binding Blade's wrists slipped just a hair. He rested his chin on his chest, pretending to be deep in thought, and pondered his strategy. At the rate he was going his arms would be almost loose in ten minutes. Should he make a bid for freedom then or wait? If he waited until they reached the estate escape might be impossible. The wisest resource was to swing into action before then.

But when?

The Warrior decided to wing it. When the right opportunity presented itself, he would know. He lifted his head and watched colorful birds frolic in the trees on a nearby small island. Approximately 100 feet to the south were several tall white birds with long, sticklike legs. They resembled cranes, but weren't. "What are those?" he asked.

Jacques shifted in his seat. "Egrets, man. Great egrets, I think." His eyes narrowed. "Where can you be from that you don't know about egrets? They are widespread in the south."

"You know, you're right. I had one as a pet when I was five but forgot all about it."

"Egrets make lousy pets. And you are a pitiful liar, *mon ami.*"

Blade focused on the distant city. "How many people live in New Orleans now?"

"About two, maybe three thousand."

"And they let the Black Snake Society walk all over them?"

"What else can they do? They're not permitted to own guns. Years ago all firearms were confiscated. And they can't stand up to Damballah with clubs and knives."

The vivid memory of that gigantic snake devouring Henri Pétion made Blade's lips curl downward. "No, they couldn't. One day, though, they'll rise in revolt."

"Never happen, man. They're sheep. They lack the courage to piss without permission."

"Someone has courage. Someone sent a distress call."

"And the message brought you here? Then you're a fool for becoming involved in matters that are none of your concern."

"Tyranny and oppression are rightfully the concern of every person who cherishes freedom."

"My, my. You would make a great Resistance fighter."

"Why won't you admit the days of the Black Snake Society are numbered? If a resistance movement has already sprung into existence, then you'll be looking for a new line of work shortly."

Jacques laughed and twirled the sunglasses in his left hand. "Keep dreaming, Dieneces."

Shrugging, Blade feigned an interest in a hawk winging high above the bayou.

"Dieneces isn't your real name, is it, man?"

"What was your first clue?"

"I've never heard such a name before. It's too—strange— to be a legitimate name."

"Dieneces was a warrior in ancient Greece."

"Where?"

"Greece. You know. The small country on the north side of the Mediterranean Sea."

"Is this sea connected to the Gulf of Mexico?"

"Not quite," Blade replied, glancing at the sergeant. "Geography isn't your strong suit, I take it."

"I don't know very much about the world," Jacques admitted. "Learning such facts is difficult when there are no books to learn from."

"What happened to all the books?"

"The Baron has a huge library at his estate, but only Majesta and him are allowed to use it. All the other books were burned many years ago."

"Ignorance is servitude, huh?"

Jacques wedged his Uzi between his knees and used both hands to place his sunglasses in his left shirt pocket. "You say the strangest things, *monsieur*. Everything about you is different. I know we've never met and yet I feel I know you. How is that possible?"

"You certainly didn't read about me in a book."

"Perhaps I've heard of you then?"

"I doubt it. I'm not famous," Blade said. He slowly curled his forearms under his seat, screening his wrists. More slack had resulted from his exertions, and he would be ready to make his move soon. "Are you married, Sergeant?"

Jacques did a double take. "What an unusual thing to ask for a man in your position. Yes, as a matter of fact, I am."

"Is your wife a member of the Black Snake Society?"

"No. She spends most of her time raising our five children. We have a modest house on Fillmore Avenue near the old City Park."

"How does she feel about you being one of the *tonton macoutes*?"

"Maylene knows I do what I must for the security of my family."

"Ahhh. So that's it. You became a member of the Society for the benefit of your loved ones. Men will often compromise their ideals if it means the ones they care for will be happier," Blade stated.

Jacques features became rigid for a bit. "I think I see what you are trying to do, giant one, and I'm not amused. You will be so kind as to keep your mouth shut for the rest of the trip unless you're spoken to. Is this understood?"

"I didn't mean to offend you."

"No, but you are trying to put dangerous thoughts in my head. You are very clever, *mon ami*. You manipulate the minds of others to your advantage, and unless they are very smart they have no idea what has been done to them."

"If you say so."

"I do," Jacques insisted testily. "Now keep your mouth shut or we will shut it for you."

Blade shrugged and resigned himself to spending the rest of the journey in silence. Actually, it didn't matter. The nylon cord was now loose enough to be shed with a sharp motion, so all he had to do was bide his time. He used the trip to rest and gird himself for the coming battle. After all he had learned about the Black Snake Society, he rated them as one of the worst postwar despotic groups. The tyranny must be brought to an end and he was just the man to do it.

Slowly the time passed. The sun sank to just above the western horizon and the air became cool due to a brisk breeze

blowing from the northwest. The drone of the outboard
motors kept most of the wildlife away from the boats,
although once an alligator 18 feet in length approached to
within ten yards of the lead craft before sharply turning aside.

A large island appeared approximately a half mile ahead.

Blade noted an expansive compound situated at the center
of the southern shoreline, almost at the water's edge, a
compound surrounded by stone walls 20 feet high. The
Baron's estate, he conjectured, and noticed the three boats
were angling toward a pier jutting into the bayou from near
an iron gate positioned in the middle of the south wall.

A dozen other boats were already docked at the pier. Many
guards, *tonton macoutes* armed with automatic weapons,
were posted on the pier or walked on the rampart at the top
of the wall.

The sight of so many enemies sparked Blade into action.
He couldn't let them get him inside. His eyes strayed to his
Bowies, still tucked under Jacques's belt, and he opted to
make his move. With a surge of his powerful shoulders he
tore his wrists from the cord and lunged, wrapping his arms
around Jacques before the stunned magician could employ
a weapon.

Together they toppled into the snake- and gator-infested
swamp.

CHAPTER FOURTEEN

Cottonmouth!

Lynx knew enough about snakes to recognize one of the deadliest species on the North American continent. He froze, his breath catching in his throat, fearing that the slightest move could provoke a strike. And once those venomous fangs sank into his flesh, once the poison began to circulate in his bloodstream, he might as well start digging his own grave.

The snake did not seem to be in any great hurry. Its head rose several inches, its tongue flicking constantly.

Lynx had to consciously suppress a shudder. He was tempted to try and kick the reptile as far as he could, but he stood perfectly still and waited for the viper to move on.

The conversation among the *tonton macoutes* continued.

"Suit yourselves," the man named Jacques said. "You are probably right to stay. The Baron would be extremely displeased if we abandoned one of our own without probable cause. Get in, Dieneces."

Lynx listened inattentively, his eyes on the cottonmouth. Come on, move! he almost roared. He couldn't understand why the stupid snake was just resting there on his feet. The odor alone should be sufficient to drive the reptile into the weeds.

His feet! His warm, sweaty feet!

Lynx stared at the conspicuous pits on both sides of the wicked-looking head, knowing they were the heat-sensitive means by which the viper located warm-blooded prey. The snake must be aware of his presence. Why hadn't it bitten him? He concluded the reptile had been moving through the weeds and slithered onto the trail and his feet before it quite realized what was happening. Now the blasted serpent was just lying there, trying to make up its pea-sized mind whether to keep going or attack.

Which figured.

Why did these things always happen to him?

He liked a little excitement as much as the next guy—no, he liked excitement a hell of a lot more than the next guy; he craved excitement, thrived on it—but this was ridiculous.

From up ahead came the voice of Jacques. "Didn't you hear me? Get in the damn boat, man."

Lynx almost hissed in frustration. Great! The *tonton macoutes* were preparing to leave and he was stuck where he stood, unable to move because of a tootsie-lovin' snake.

"Sit in the middle."

What should he do? To be thwarted by a measly serpent galled Lynx intensely, and his anger fought with his innate dread of all snakes for supremacy. If he didn't do something soon, he'd be up a creek with a paddle. Or was that up a bayou without a boat? Unless the pair who were staying had one.

"Not you two! Only one of you to a boat. There is less chance of you giving us trouble."

Lynx deduced the man must be referring to Ferret and Gremlin. He recalled the name mentioned a minute ago and his brow furrowed in perplexity. Who the heck was Dieneces?

Suddenly the cottonmouth moved.

Lynx grinned when he felt the reptile's scales sliding across his toes, and he glanced down, craning his neck to see over

Eleanore's unconscious form, expecting to see the snake on its way to parts unknown.

Instead, the cottonmouth was wrapping itself around his right ankle.

Just when he thought his predicament couldn't possibly get any worse! Lynx scowled and watched the serpent make itself right at home, coiling around his leg until its entire length, except for the head resting on the top of his foot and the tip of tail dangling from the rear, was looped about his ankle. Mentally he vented a dozen oaths.

"You don't look very happy, *mon ami.*"

"It's all this air pollution."

"Beg pardon?"

"When was the last time you took a bath?"

Lynx smiled at the giant's quip, but the smile died on his lips a moment later when the snake began rubbing its snout against his foot.

Now what?

Fascinated, Lynx stared at the reptile until it stopped and lifted its head four or five inches to gaze around. An idea occurred to him and he slowly eased his chest lower. Since he was already bent over at the waist, his hands were within half a foot of the serpent's noodle. If he could just ease down—

The roar of outboard motors being started shattered the stillness of the swamp, and the noise rose in volume as the motors were revved.

Lynx glanced toward the water. The weeds screened the shore, hiding the boats from view. He listened in mounting chagrin to the motors as the craft headed eastward. If he didn't get his butt in gear, he'd lose them. Uncharacteristically anxious, he resumed lowering his hands toward the cottonmouth. In another minute, if the snake didn't move, he'd teach the reptile to mess with his tootsies.

At the raucous sound of the outboards the serpent had elevated its head another inch.

Smirking at his impending victory, Lynx had to crane his

neck even farther to keep his eyes on the unwanted hitchhiker.

The cottonmouth, oblivious to the danger, stared eastward, its tongue flicking.

Got you now, you suck-egg slimebucket! Lynx thought, and paused with his right hand within three inches of the reptile's head. He tensed to make the final lunge.

Abruptly, without any warning, Eleanore groaned and shifted in his arms.

Lynx almost lost his balance. He had to grip her with all of his strength so she wouldn't fall, and he inadvertently shuffled a half-pace forward.

Oh, no!

The blood seemed to pound in his temples as he stiffened in anticipation of being bitten. He looked down at the snake.

The cottonmouth was gazing up at him.

Uh-oh.

Lynx stared into the reptile's unblinking eyes and felt a chill ripple along his spine. Perhaps it was only his imagination, but he intuitively sensed the serpent knew that its body was wrapped around a leg and not a sapling. The next few moments would be critical.

The cottonmouth suddenly opened its mouth wide, exposing the lighter-colored lining on the inside for which it had been named, and its fangs. Normally tucked back along the jaw, the fangs of a viper were designed so they would swing forward when the mouth was open.

Lynx swallowed and riveted his gaze on that deadly maw, his dread becoming outright apprehension at the realization he was powerless to prevent the snake from biting.

A heartbeat later the cottonmouth closed its mouth.

Eleanore moaned again.

Lynx couldn't afford to put off the inevitable any longer. The reptile might strike at any second. He saw the head begin to tilt toward his leg and he went into action, sweeping his right hand downward, knowing if he missed he was dead. Because Eleanore partly blocked his view, he had to rely on his finely honed instincts and hope his hand closed on the right spot. There was no margin for error.

The serpent's mouth started to open again.

Do it!

Lynx's hand clamped onto the cottonmouth at the base of its jaw. He felt the cool scales on his palm, where the fur was thinner than almost anywhere else on his body, and squeezed, gritting his teeth as his sinews went as rigid as steel.

The reptile snapped the air, then attempted to bite his leg.

Lynx increased the pressure, exerting himself to his limit and beyond, feeling the neck and head collapse and squish between his fingers. Still he strangled the serpent, unwilling to relent for an instant. The thick rope of a form lashed and whipped his ankles as it wound and unwound, hissing all the while.

Die, damn you!

Eleanore tried to turn over, causing his arms to slacken. He almost lost his grip.

Dingbat!

The thrashing and convulsing halted unexpectedly and the cottonmouth went limp.

Lynx expelled a long breath and straightened, raising the serpent for a closer inspection. The snake's eyes were bulging from their sockets and its red tongue hung from its parted lips.

Got you!

Uttering a soft groan, Eleanore awakened and glanced blankly around as if she couldn't comprehend the situation in which she found herself. "Who—?" she said, and happened to look at the crushed snake in his hand.

"Done taking your nap?" Lynx joked.

Eleanore's lips moved, she voiced a plaintive squeak, and fainted.

"Yo-yo," Lynx muttered, and was about to cast the cottonmouth from him when he heard the distinctive metallic click of a submachine gun cocking handle being pulled back. He looked up.

There were two of them, *tonton macoutes* in their traditional black uniforms and mirrored sunglasses. They had their weapons trained on him.

"Look at what we have here," declared the skinny man on the right. "A snake-killer."

"Another freak, man," said the second one.

"You wouldn't win any beauty contest yourself, pal," Lynx responded arrogantly.

"And it talks!" exclaimed the skinny man.

"What's a beauty contest?" inquired the other.

"They hold them in the Civilized Zone," Lynx explained. "Once a year they have a Miss Civilized Zone Contest. A lot of human broads with big boobs prance across a stage in a bathing suit and wiggle their fannies for drooling judges. Sort of pitiful, if you ask me. They don't even issue napkins to the judges."

"You're jerking us around, man," the skinny man declared.

"What do we do with them, Louis?"

"What else, Alex?" the skinny man rejoined. "We take them to the Baron."

Lynx took a step toward them, almost laughing when they backpedaled a few feet and hefted their weapons.

"Don't move!" Louis barked.

"Not unless you all want to look like a sieve," Alex addded.

"I just want to put this dingbat down. My arms are gettin' tired," Lynx stated.

"Tough, man," Louis said. "You can carry her to the bayou, then set her down." He backed up and motioned with his barrel for Lynx to follow.

"Let's go," Alex prompted, staying next to his companion.

Lynx dutifully walked after them, the snake clutched in

his hand. The serpent might come in handy, he decided. "I suppose my buddies are long gone, huh?"

"Those other freaks and the big one are your friends?" Alex said. "To be expected. And yes, they are out of sight by now. But don't fret. In a couple of hours you'll be reunited."

Louis snickered. "For the last time."

Lynx plastered a patently phony smile on his mouth and walked along the trail for 15 feet until he came to a narrow strip of shore bordering the swamp. To his right, pulled partly onto the soft ground, rested a boat.

"Now you can place the woman at your feet," Louis stated.

"Slowly, man," mentioned Alex. "And no tricks or we will blow you away."

"You guys must be terrors at a party," Lynx cracked. He knelt and gingerly deposited Eleanore on the soil, then paused, his right hand next to his leg. "Poor kid has been through a lot," he said, and glanced at the *tonton macoutes*. "I don't suppose either of you morons would have any food?"

"Don't be insulting us, freak," Louis snapped.

"She'll eat when we reach the estate, if then," Alex remarked.

"The woman is starving," Lynx said.

Louis chuckled. "Should we cry now or later?"

Straightening slowly, Lynx moved his right arm behind his knee, the snake rubbing against his calf. "Okay. How do you want to play this?"

"First we will bind you," Louis announced. He reached into his right pants pocket and withdrew a black nylon cord.

"Just happen to have one of those with you?" Lynx quipped good-naturedly.

"We are required to apprehend enemies of the Black Snake Society wherever we find them. Besides, there aren't enough handcuffs to go around," Louis divulged.

"Maybe I'll get you a pair for your birthday if you treat me nice."

"You and Dieneces both don't know when to shut up, do you?"

"Die-e-who?"

"Don't play games with us. Your big friend, the one with all the muscles."

"Oh. Yeah. Dieneces. How could I forget him?"

Louis approached cautiously to within a foot of the hybrid. "Hold out your arms, palms pressed together," he ordered.

"Are you sure you want me to do this?" Lynx said, stalling, sliding a few inches to his left to put Louis between him and Alex.

"Do it, this second, or I'll blow your balls off."

"Hey, go easy on the jewels, pal. And if that's the way you want to be—" Lynx stated, and whipped his arms up, extending them toward Louis and hurling the dead cottonmouth at the man's face.

Startled, Louis instinctively recoiled in alarm.

And Lynx pounced.

CHAPTER
FIFTEEN

Blade had slanted to the right as he leaped, intending to come down in the water on the south side of the boat, well clear of the outboard. But he hadn't counted on Jacques suddenly resisting just as they went over the edge, causing them to roll as they went under, to sink directly under the craft. He released the sergeant, grabbed his Bowies, and kicked to put distance between himself and the *tonton macoutes* up above.

Jacques did the opposite. In his haste to get away from the giant, he stroked for the surface and neglected to look overhead to ensure the boat had completely passed by.

A fatal mistake.

The Warrior saw the propeller catch the sergeant in the top of the head, the blades shearing through his cranium as if his skull was so much putty, sending a stream of hair, bone fragments, pulpy brain matter, and blood into the bayou.

Jacques only convulsed once, then sagged, his arms and legs limp.

Blade twisted and dived deeper, anticipating the next move of the men in the boats. The water was cool and murky, but he could see the bottom less than eight feet below. Thankful he had taken a deep breath before going under, he swam down another six feet, then reversed direction and headed under the boats.

The *tonton macoutes* had stopped their craft. The muted blasting of high-powered weapons broke out, and dozens of rounds zipped into the bayou.

Blade glanced down and saw the thin trails of the bullets crisscrossing the water. The men in black were concentrating their fire to the south, where he had last been seen. He swam onward, bearing to the north, wondering if his lungs would hold out long enough for him to reach cover.

The frenzied firing went on unabated.

His arms and legs cleaving the water smoothly, Blade put ten yards behind him. Then 15. And 20. His chest began to ache, but he ignored the pain and kept pumping his limbs rhythmically.

Thirty yards.

Forty.

The Warrior could feel the pressure building in his lungs, and the pangs became sharper, almost unbearable. He angled upward, slowing as he neared the surface, and it took all of his considerable self-control to refrain from gasping loudly for air when he finally stuck his head up. He inhaled deeply, yet quietly, and seldom had he treasured the simple experience of breathing as he did now.

The shooting had ceased.

Blade looked at the craft and saw the *tonton macoutes* searching the water in the vicinity of the boats. Two of them were fishing Jacques from the bayou.

Ferret and Gremlin were seated on their respective craft, both leaning forward intently. The humanoid happened to glance to the north.

Blade wanted to wave, but the motion might be seen by the *tonton macoutes*. He knew the hybrids possessed remarkable eyesight, so he simply grinned and winked and submerged again. With the Bowies still clutched in his hands he stroked on, losing track of the distance, seeking a temporary sanctuary. Reinforcements were bound to arrive from the estate at any minute and a massive manhunt would undoubtedly be launched.

He had no intention of being caught again.

The Warrior swam for another 15 minutes, surfacing when necessary to inhale fresh air, skirting solitary trees and isolated mounds of dense vegetation. Twice he saw snakes. Neither came within striking range. And once he saw an alligator, a small one less than six feet in length swimming from east to west. The reptile never paid any attention to him.

The underside of an island appeared ahead, approximately 70 yards wide.

Blade made for the rather steep bank, rising to the surface when he was 20 yards away. He discovered the island was not much larger than an acre in all and covered with thickets and cypress trees, a perfect spot to hide out until nightfall. He spied a limb jutting downward near the water and made for it.

Brightly colored finches flew by overhead.

In a minute the Warrior came within reach of the limb and paused, dog-paddling, about to slide the Bowies into their sheaths. Out of the corner of his left eye he detected movement, and he glanced around to discover a large black snake bearing down on him, not six feet off.

There was no time to determine if the serpent was poisonous or not.

Blade lifted both Bowies and hacked at the snake the second it came close enough. The keen edges penetrated its head, splitting the reptile open. A second swipe of his right hand decapitated the reptile.

The sinuous body continued to writhe and thrash despite the absence of its brain.

Blade quickly wiped the knives on his pants, placed them in their sheaths, and grabbed the limb. Another moment saw him safely out of the water and stepping onto dry land. He turned to stare to the south.

The boats were no longer in sight.

Good.

He pivoted and scrutinized the vegetation all around him. If the *tonton macoutes* came this far, he'd be difficult to find. If they didn't, once darkness settled he planned to head for the estate of Baron Laveau. He disliked the idea of being separated from the hybrids, but he'd had no choice.

Something rustled in the brush.

Blade rested his hands on his Bowies, thinking of the huge snake known as Damballah. Where did the creature hole up when not on the prowl? Of all the animals in the bayou, he felt confident he could handle every one with just his knives except the so-called Snake God. His Bowies would hardly make a dent in such a tremendous abberation of nature. Yet the thing must be killed.

But how?

How could he slay such an awesome monstrosity?

The Warrior shook his head and walked inland, parting the undergrowth with his forearms, treading carefully, constantly on the alert for snakes. When he had traversed a dozen yards a thin green form slithered off to the east. Minutes later he spied a rabbit bounding away.

Shortly the shadows began to lengthen as the sun dipped partly below the horizon.

Blade came to a wide clearing. Lying in the center was a large log, the slowly rotting remnant of a once-towering tree. He walked over and sat down, relieved at the opportunity to rest and formulate his strategy.

Birds sang in the nearby woods. Insects buzzed noisily.

Long minutes dragged by without any sound of pursuit.

The serene setting lulled Blade into a sense of complacency. He thought of Jenny and Gabe, wishing with all of his soul that he would be with them soon. First things first, however. Eradicating the Black Snake Society was paramount. He speculated on whether simply terminating the Baron would suffice to end the *tonton macoutes,* and he concluded they would probably appoint another leader or one would merely take over where the Baron had left off. So killing the Baron wasn't enough. He must exterminate the entire Society in order to free the people of New Orleans. Considering the odds, the task promised to be formidable.

Maybe the key lay in Damballah.

The huge snake was more than a mere symbol of the Black Snake Society's power; it was their Deity Incarnate, tangible proof of their masterful magic, physical evidence of the efficacy of their voodoo. Their living god rendered them invincible in their own eyes and cowed the populace of New Orleans. If Damballah could be destroyed, if someone could prove the Black Snake Society wasn't omnipotent, their days would be numbered.

Which brought him back to square one.

How do you kill a snake bigger than a killer whale?

Blade put his hands on the log and stared thoughtfully at the grass, mulling his options. His ears registered a faint scraping noise to his rear, but he paid no attention to the sound. Absorbed in contemplation, he racked his brain for a means of slaying Damballah. A machine gun might do the trick, provided the gun fired at point-blank range and the snake stayed still long enough to take a few dozen rounds in the head. A hand grenade would definitely do the job, but he didn't have one.

The scraping noise intruded on his reflection again, only louder this time.

Idly curious, Blade shifted and looked behind him. The moment he laid eyes on the creature stalking him and saw its iron jaws spread wide to chomp on his back, he threw himself forward into a smooth roll and rose with his Bowies out and ready.

On the far side of the log, its squat bulk supported by four stout legs, its head extended and its tapered mouth all the way open, its spiteful brown eyes glaring at him in inexplicable primal rage, stood a snapping turtle four feet in height at the curved crest of its shell.

Blade marveled at the animal's size and slowly backed away. With the log interposed between them, he felt safe. The turtle's head came even with the top of the fallen tree, but its legs were too short to push it over.

The snapper hissed.

"I didn't know this island was occupied," Blade quipped, and halted eight feet from the log. In the bayou, it seemed, a person couldn't turn his back for a second. He studied the reptile, estimating it to be three times the normal size, yet another example of radiation- or chemical-induced giantism. If he hadn't looked back when he did, the thing would now be tearing him to shreds and gulping his flesh down. Thank the Spirit turtles were notoriously slow!

A rustling came from his right.

Blade glanced in that direction and saw another snapper coming toward him. It moved ponderously, and he could easily outrun the animal.

More rustling came from the left.

Goose bumps broke out on the Warrior's skin as he observed two more snappers lumbering toward him. What in the world was going on? Had he stumbled onto their breeding island? He pivoted, decided to get away from the clearing, and there were three more spaced about a yard apart and charging in their own lethargic fashion.

The largest of freshwater species, snappers were renowned for their fierce dispositions and jaws like steel traps. Distinguished by massive heads, long tails, and heavy carapices, snappers would eat anything they could catch.

Blade decided to beat a hasty retreat. He spun to the east and ran straight at the lone snapper blocking his path. The turtle extended its neck as far as it could go, eager to rip into him. But at the last second he leaped, arcing five feet into the air and sailing over the snapper, its jaws snapping shut within inches of his combat boots. He landed lightly and chuckled, then darted into the vegetation bordering the clearing.

And promptly realized he had only compounded his problem.

There were many more snappers lurking in the weeds and thickets, dozens of them all around him.

The Warrior darted aside as a head lanced at him from out of a clump of high grass. He ran a few yards and was compelled to dodge to the left when another turtle materialized in front of him.

A universal, irate hissing broke out.

Blade paused, seeking a safe avenue through the snappers. None existed. His best bet was to keep moving, to run the gauntlet of vicious jaws as quickly as he could. Instantly he took off, sprinting in short steps, wary of accidentally blundering into one of the ponderous reptiles.

A small snapper appeared on the left and bit at him.

Blade darted to the right, nimbly skirting a partly concealed snapper, and ran due east for five yards before he was compelled to dance to the left once again.

And so it went.

For over five minutes Blade weaved and twisted and side-stepped as never before, evading gaping mouth after gaping mouth, listening to the constant hissing and the loud snap of the powerful jaws that could rend him as easily as if his body was made of soft clay. The darkening shadows complicated his escape, distorting his perception, causing him to go even slower than he might otherwise have gone. His legs began to tire, his reflexes to slow.

How many more were there?

Aware a single misstep could cause his death, Blade dashed to the north to avoid a squat shape, and only after he passed it did he realize he had just successfully avoided the stump of a tree.

Now his mind was playing tricks on him!

The Warrior covered eight more yards. Abruptly, the snappers dwindled. He found himself on a narrow strip of clear land on the east side of the island, the water not ten feet away, and halted, glancing right and left.

Not a turtle in sight.

Overjoyed at his deliverance, Blade slid the Bowies back in their sheaths and gazed at the underbrush behind him, waiting to see if the snappers would pursue him. After 30 seconds he judged himself to be safe, so he focused his attention on the twilight-enshrouded bayou.

The harsh whine of an outboard unexpectedly shattered the stillness, and around the southeast corner of the island sped a boat filled with armed *tonton macoutes*.

CHAPTER SIXTEEN

The bozos were candy.

Lynx took out the first one, Louis, with a swipe of his rigid nails, tearing the man's throat open from side to side before Louis could recover from the shock of having the cottonmouth hurled at him. He shoved, sending Louis backwards, causing the *tonton macoute* to stumble into Alex.

The second man in black endeavored to push his friend aside and aim at the hybrid, but he found his human reflexes were no match for the uncanny speed of the cat-man.

Lynx darted around Louis and swatted Alex's weapon aside with his left forearm. His right hand streaked to Alex's neck and clamped tight, and with a surge of his shoulder and arm muscles he lifted Alex clear off the ground, pivoted, and slammed the man down.

Alex gamely tried to bring his weapon into play.

Not today, chump! Lynx thought, and lashed out with his right foot, catching Alex on the temple, stunning the *tonton macoute*. A second kick, planted on the tip of Alex's chin, rendered the man in black unconscious.

What a couple of wimps!

Lynx looked at Louis, who convulsed wildly on the dank earth, then stepped over and knelt beside Eleanore. A hasty check verified the woman was still out like a light. Her skin felt extremely hot to the touch, a certain indication of a fever. Which annoyed him no end. As if he didn't have enough to worry about, now she required medical attention.

The old saying was right.

When it rained, it poured.

Lynx lifted Eleanore and deposited her in the boat. He collected the fallen weapons, an M-16 and an M3A1 sub-machine gun, and stripped the *tonton macoutes* of the ammo they carried in pouches attached to the rear of their belts. The weaponry went in the boat, and a moment later he was pushing the boat into the water. He undid the line, reached for the outboard, and paused.

Alex groaned and struggled to his elbows, blood trickling from his mouth. He looked at Louis, then at the boat. "Stop!"

"You've *got* to be kiddin' turkey," Lynx replied, and lowered his right hand to the submachine gun.

"If it's the last thing I ever do, man, I'll kill you," Alex vowed, trying to rise.

"Afraid not, chuckles. You've got it all backwards," Lynx told him. "And don't bother getting up on my account." He raised the M3A1, worked the cocking handle, and fired.

Alex's eyes widened the instant the weapon appeared. He scrambled feebly away from the bayou, but he had gone only a yard when the submachine gun chattered and the .45-caliber rounds smashed into his torso and flattened him on his back in a growing puddle of his own blood.

"Since you're a magician, maybe you can bring yourself back to life," Lynx remarked to the corpse, and placed the submachine gun at his feet. He experimented with the outboard, adjusting the throttle and turning the small gray key before the motor kicked over. A satisfied smile creased his lips. He'd driven vehicles with manual chokes on many occasions, and the outboard was no different.

Eleanore shifted but didn't awaken.

Frowning, concerned for her welfare, Lynx revved the motor and headed out across the murky water. He had no idea in which direction the *tonton macoutes* had taken Blade, Ferret, and Gremlin. His best bet, therefore, called for heading to New Orleans, where he could find assistance for Eleanore and hopefully elicit information concerning the Baron's estate.

Only the top rim of the sun was visible to the west.

Lynx made himself as comfortable as he could and stared straight ahead, fascinated by the swampy domain so different from any he had ever seen. Birds were everywhere. So were snakes. He saw many before the darkness encroached enough to limit visibility. The descent of nightfall posed an inconvenience. There were countless isolated trees and mounds and logs dotting the bayou. Hitting any one of them would send the boat to the bottom. If it became too dark, he'd have to pick his way slowly or go on foot. And with Eleanore unconscious, walking was impractical. Not to mention unhealthy, what with all the damn snakes.

Lynx had been able to fix the position of the city in his mind before it became too dark to see the former metropolis, and he relied on his unerring feline instincts to guide him once it did. Lacking a watch, he had to estimate the passage of time and distance, and initially he calculated New Orleans to be four or five miles away. He also assumed the bayou would take him directly to the outskirts, but after progressing only two miles, and just as twilight began to give way to the deeper inkiness of night, he spied land ahead.

What was this?

He stood in the boat for a better view, surprised to discover the land was actually that: the mainland, not a mere island. An ancient pier jutted into the water, extending 50 feet from the bank, and four other boats were tied at dock. None of them resembled the type of boats used by the *tonton macoutes*. Beyond the pier a paved road led off to the east.

Lynx directed the boat toward the land, wondering if he would be able to locate a functional vehicle he could "borrow" to transport Eleanore into the city. Movement below a stand of trees near the pier arrested his attention, and he stared at the spot for a second before his sharp eyes recognized the shape of the tethered horse.

Wow!

Maybe he did have a guardian angel like the Elders claimed.

Chuckling at his good luck, Lynx brought the boat in next to the end of the pier. He cut the outboard and grabbed hold of the narrow ladder leading upward from the water. Working rapidly, he secured the boat to the pier, and was bending to lift Eleanore when an unexpected sound stiffened him in consternation.

Someone coughed.

Lynx leaped to the ladder and climbed to the top. As he cleared the rim he was amazed to behold an elderly man sitting 15 feet off, fishing from the edge of the pier. The man's dark clothing blended into the darkness, rendering him almost invisible except at close range.

"Hi, there."

The friendly greeting was the last thing Lynx expected. He straightened warily and walked toward the thin figure. "Hey, mister. How's it hanging?"

"Oh, about nine inches."

Lynx halted in surprise, then cackled. "Nine inches! I like that. Almost as big as mine."

The fisherman regarded Lynx with an air of curious fascination. He wore jeans and a blue shirt, both of which had seen their prime decades ago. His receding hairline gave him a distinguished aspect. "Sounds like you've got a regular snake in your drawers."

"Do me a favor and don't talk about snakes," Lynx said, moving forward.

"Do you mind if I ask you a question?"

"Not at all, Gramps. Shoot."

"What the hell *are* you?"

"You ever heard of mutations?"

"Who hasn't? But I ain't never heard of one that could talk. Where are you from?"

"Would you believe Mars?"

"Nope. I heard about them octopuses when I was a whippersnapper. We kicked their keisters but good."

"You too, huh?"

"What?"

"Nothin'. What's your name, gramps?"

"Bob. Bob Wells."

"Do you live around here?"

"Just down the road a piece."

Lynx nodded at the horse. "Is that yours?"

"Yep. I call him Saddlesore. Had him for going on eleven years."

"I need to borrow him."

Bob Wells placed his fishing pole by his left leg. "I don't know as how I'd like that."

"It's not for me," Lynx explained. He started toward the end of the pier. "Come here a sec."

"What for?" Wells responded suspiciously.

"I want to show you something."

"I don't know."

Lynx stopped and put a friendly smile on his face. "Look, if I wanted to harm you, you'd already be dead. There's a woman here who needs to see a doctor, and fast."

Wells slowly stood, his head cocked to one side, eyeing the hybrid skeptically. "A woman?"

"Yeah. See for yourself." Lynx stepped to the south side of the pier, giving the elderly man plenty of room to pass. "I won't move."

"I guess I can trust you," Wells stated with the same degree of confidence he might use in referring to a ravenous gator. He edged cautiously to the end and peered over the side.

"Well?" Lynx prompted.

"I'll be damned. You were telling the truth. Who is she?"

"Her name is Eleanore DeCoud."

"What happened to her? Did you hurt her?"

"Me?" Lynx snapped, and moved over beside the oldster. "Are you crazy? I don't make a habit of beatin' up on bimbos. The *tonton macoutes* were after her and—" he began, and was immediately interrupted.

"Those bastards! They did this to her?"

"More or less. She's a member of the Resistance."

Wells gaped at Eleanore, then reached out to touch the hybrid's arm. "Hell, man. If she's with the Resistance, you can keep my horse. Do what you need to."

"Thanks," Lynx said. He hurried down the ladder to get her.

"Those vermin killed my boy about fourteen years ago," Wells detailed. "If I was a bit younger I'd be with the Resistance myself. There's a lot of us who would jump at the chance to do what we can to help them."

Lynx draped Eleanore over his left shoulder and began the ascent. "You're not gettin' any younger, Gramps. What have you got to lose if you join them now?"

The question caused Wells to think for a moment before answering. "Nothing but my life. What little is left of it."

"Like I said. What have you got to lose?" Lynx stressed. He came over the top and accepted a hand of assistance from the fisherman. "Thanks."

"Come on. I'll make sure you get on Saddlesore," Wells offered, hastening toward the stand of trees.

"Do you think your horse will spook? Some horses aren't able to handle being ridden by someone who smells like an animal."

"There's just one way to find out."

Lynx cradled Eleanore in his arms and followed. "Where's the nearest doctor?"

"Do you mean like in the old days? Hell, man, there ain't none of them around anymore. The smartest thing you can do is get your lady-friend to Marie. Her place is about a mile and a half from here. Marie will have your friend on her feet in no time."

"Is this Marie a nurse or an herbal healer?"

"Nope. Marie is a *mambo*."

"What's that?"

"She practices voodoo."

Lynx abruptly halted. "Are you out of your gourd, gramps? Didn't you hear me? Those voodoo types are out to kill this woman."

"Not Marie," Wells said, pausing. "Marie practices good voodoo, the kind that heals people, not the black magic practiced by the Black Snake Society."

"Are you sure it's safe for us to go there?"

"Trust me. Marie has been helping the folks in these parts for damn near thirty years. She's the salt of the earth."

"If you say so."

Wells continued to his horse. The animal shied and he had to grip the reins tightly to prevent it from fleeing. "Whoa, boy! What's the matter with you?"

"It's me," Lynx said from six feet away. "I was afraid of this."

"Do you want a suggestion?"

"Anything."

"Put the woman down and climb on Saddlesore. If you can show him who's boss, he'll let you ride him, no problem."

Lynx hesitated. Trying to break in the animal seemed like a monumental waste of time. But if he succeeded, he'd get to the *mambo's* place that much sooner. "All right," he said, and gently lowered Eleanore down once more.

"Just climb right up," Wells advised, straining on the reins.

"Climb, hell," Lynx declared. He took two steps and sprang, his wiry form gracefully sailing through the air to come down squarely in the saddle. The horse seemed to freeze. ''This might be easier than I thought,'' he remarked, and took the reins.

He spoke too soon.

Saddlesore suddenly erupted into violent motion, bucking and twisting like the wildest mustang that ever lived, reverting to the instinctual level of its evolutionary ancestors, neighing all the while.

Lynx clamped his legs on the horse and held onto the reins with all of his strength, his body jarred by every buck and wrenched by every twist. He had only limited experience riding horses, and none whatsoever at breaking the animals in. Still, he felt confident his feline prowess would enable him to weather the equine storm.

Saddlesore moved away from the trees and into the middle of the road, his legs stiff, his back arched, bucking even harder and higher.

The world spun before Lynx's eyes, a vague swirl of shadowy contours. He thought he heard Wells yelling at him but the words were indistinct. His complete concentration was devoted to the task of staying on the horse. Never, ever would he allow a dumb animal to defeat him, so he clung to Saddlesore tenaciously and endured agonizing torment in the process. Time stood still. He had no idea whether he rode the horse for three minutes or ten. Gradually, his legs began to tire and his arms to ache.

Then the light appeared.

Lynx didn't know what to make of the bright light that suddenly enveloped both the animal and himself. The brilliant whitish glow grew brighter and brighter, dazzling his eyes when the horse turned in a certain direction.

Somewhere, Bob Wells shouted muddied words.

Lynx had about had enough. The combination of the strange illumination and the shouting convinced him something must be wrong. He prepared to vault from Saddlesore, but in the second before he leaped, the steed abruptly and astonishingly stopped in its tracks, wheezing in great gasps.

"Congratulations!" someone cried out in a gruff voice, and clapped in appreciation.

For a moment Lynx experienced disorientation. He was facing directly toward the source of the lights, which he now recognized as the twin headlights of a military-style convoy truck parked only 20 feet off. And he also perceived another chilling fact.

Tonton macoutes completely surrounded him.

CHAPTER SEVENTEEN

"I don't care what you say. I'm going to kill him."

"Ferret is joking, yes?"

"Nope."

"But you can't be serious, no? Lynx is our friend."

"Some friend. He's the idiot who talked us into this, remember? Maybe you can overlook a few minor incidents like being shot at, almost being gobbled up by a jumbo snake, being beaten with a gun barrel, and then captured by refugees from a psycho farm," Ferret declared angrily. "I can't."

"Gremlin has a better idea, yes," the humanoid said. "Just punch Lynx in the mouth."

"After I skin him alive and boil him in oil."

Gremlin sighed and walked to the small barred window in their cell. He gazed out at the bayou and pier, both 40 yards from the tower in which they were imprisoned, and remembered the walk up from the boat several hours before. Night had fallen, and spotlights positioned at regular intervals along the outer wall illuminated both the inner grounds and the surrounding swamp. "Look at the bright side, Ferret. At least our wrists aren't tied, no?"

Seated on the sole piece of furniture in the ten-by-twelve-foot room, Ferret snorted. "Remind me to boil you with him."

"How much longer do you think they will hold us here, yes?"

"Who knows?" Ferret responded irritably.

"You must learn to control your temper, no? Sometimes you can be as bad as Lynx."

"We can't all be saints like you."

The humanoid looked at his friend. "Why are you being so rude to Gremlin? You're mad at Lynx, yes?"

Ferret detected the hurt tone in Gremlin's voice and glanced up, frowning in displeasure at his own juvenile behavior. "Good point. I shouldn't be taking out my anger at that turnip on you. I apologize."

"Gremlin understand."

"All this waiting is getting to me," Ferret groused. He stood and crossed to the locked steel door on the opposite side of the cell from the window. Standing on tiptoe, he peered through the narrow slot positioned at human eye level. A limited stretch of corridor was within his line of vision. "Still no sign of any guards."

"There's a bright side to that too, no?" Gremlin mentioned.

"How do you figure?"

"As long as they leave us alone, we stay alive, yes?"

Ferret tu rned, his lips curled wryly. "What's with all this bright-side stuff?"

"Do you like Gremlin's new and improved attitude on life, no?" the humanoid asked proudly.

"Is that what you call it?"

"Certainly, yes. Gremlin read a fascinating book in the Family library that has changed Gremlin's whole life around."

"Alice in Wonderland?"

"No. Gremlin has not read that one. Gremlin was referring to the wonderful book by the great man Peale. Have you read it?''

"Can't say that I have.''

"You really should, yes. The book will improve your life for the better, Ferret. It will give you a new lease on living, no?''

"Do you mean I'll start thinking and acting like you?''

"Yes.'' Gremlin squared his shoulders and nodded vigorously. "You will have a genuinely positive attitude about everything, yes?''

"I think I'll pass.''

"But why, no?''

"If we were meant to only look at the bright side of things, we wouldn't have the capacity to cry.''

Gremlin did a double take, his forehead furrowing, tremendously impressed by the statement. "That's beautiful, yes? Gremlin had no idea you are such a philosopher, no?''

"Don't start.''

"Start what, yes?'' Gremlin replied, then repeated the insight in a very profound manner. "If we were meant to only look at the bright side of things, we wouldn't have the capacity to cry. How wonderful, no?''

Ferret shook his head wistfully. "I think I'll shoot Lynx first, then punch him in the mouth, then skin him and boil him in oil,'' he muttered.

"What was that, yes?''

"Just talking to myself.''

"About what, no? Gremlin doesn't want to miss another word you say, yes?''

"It's not important.''

"Tell Gremlin, please?''

His shoulders slumping in resignation, Ferret gestured and stated the first thing that came into his head. "What goes around, comes around,'' he said.

The humanoid beamed broadly. "Wow! You've done it again, yes?''

"Give me a break. The humans say that expression all the time. Surely you've heard it before?''

"Gremlin doesn't think so, no."

"Well, it's not original. So don't make a big deal out of it."

"What goes around, comes around," Gremlin intoned solemnly. "Maybe you should write a book, yes?"

"Maybe I should stick a grenade down Lynx's loincloth."

"Why do you keep carping about Lynx, no?"

"You wouldn't understand."

"Try me, yes?"

"I don't—" Ferret began, then stopped when he heard the drumming of hard soles in the corridor. He spun toward the door. "We have company."

Gremlin moved over beside his companion. "Do we fight or not, no?"

"We'll go along with them for the time being. Maybe, if we play our cards right, we can lull these dimwits into lowering their guard long enough for us to make a break for it."

Where would we go, yes? We're in the middle of a swamp, no?"

"Don't bother me with technicalities. Do I have to do all the thinking for us?"

Before the humanoid could answer, the metallic grating of the bolt being thrown sounded from the far side of the steel door. An instant later a tall *tonton macoute* stood framed in the doorway. He carried an Uzi, and his sunglasses were hooked into the top pocket on the left side of his shirt. "Hello," he greeted them coldly. "I am Captain François."

"Is it time for our supper?" Ferret asked. "We're starved. Bring on the food."

"Cute," Captain François said. "Very cute." He backed into the corridor. "Now you will be so kind as to step out here with your arms over your head. No tricks or we will slay you where you stand. *Comprenez-vous?*"

"What?" Ferret responded.

"Do you understand?"

"What's not to understand? If we so much as fart, your

goons will blow us away," Ferret stated, and elevated his hands. He stepped into the corridor and discovered eight *tonton macoutes* standing to his left, their weapons trained on his chest. None of them were wearing their mirrored glasses. "Hi there, guys. Have you missed us?"

"Enjoy your humor while you can," Captain François said. "Soon you will not have much to laugh at."

"Promises, promises."

Gremlin came out of the cell and stopped next to Ferret. "Where are you taking us, yes?"

"The Baron and Majesta want to see you," Captain François divulged. "They're very curious about you freaks."

"Why would they be interested in us when they already have you around?" Ferret cracked.

The officer's eyes narrowed and he scrutinized Ferret from head to toe. "You've got a big mouth for such a little turd."

"The better to rip your throat out with, Grandma, when I get the chance."

"Which you never will," Captain François assured him mockingly. He motioned at one of the men behind him. "Bind them."

Under the steady barrels of their captors' guns, the hybrids were compelled to submit to having their wrists bound with nylon cord once again.

"And now," Captain François said when the chore had been completed, "you will come with us. Be forewarned that if you try to escape, you will be shot. And even if we should, by some fluke, miss you, there is no way you could cross the inner grounds without being nailed by one of the guards on the walls. So I trust you will behave."

"We don't intend to commit suicide," Ferret remarked.

"How nice. It would be a shame to deprive us of such magnificent entertainment." Captain François pivoted and started along the corridor.

Ferret kept silent as the *tonton macoutes* hemmed Gremlin and him in, with four men in black in front and another quartet bringing up the rear. He fumed, though. Fumed at letting Lynx talk him into going on the run, fumed at being captured, and fumed at life in general. He paid particular attention to his surroundings, hoping to detect a weakness in the fortifications that he could exploit to make good his escape.

The corridor led to a winding metal stairway, which in turn brought them from the seventh floor to ground level. As they descended, passing the lower hallways en route, moans, cries, and a few screams attended their passage.

"What was that?" Ferret inquired after a high-pitched screech emanated from the third floor.

"One of our other prisoners," the officers replied.

"How many are you holding?"

"I don't really know," Captain François admitted with transparent disinterest. "The number varies all the time. Today I believe there are fifty-seven."

"That many," Ferret blurted.

"Our prison tower can accommodate seventy-five at full capacity," François boasted.

"Your men must be slacking off."

"As a matter of fact, they have been. But the Baron intends to whip them into shape with his speech tonight."

"A regular humanitarian, huh?"

"The Baron is the latest in a long line of illustrious leaders of the Black Snake Society. Your petty mind can't begin to comprehend the magnitude of his greatness."

"I just hope I don't step in any of it on the way to wherever we're going."

From the prison tower they walked due north toward the stately mansion occupying the very middle of the estate, a four-story white affair replete with an ostentatious portico. The glare from a score of floodlights illuminated their party with a brilliance equivalent of daylight.

"Where do you get your power, yes?" Gremlin queried.

"Generators," Captain François said. "We have scoured the countryside for a hundred miles around and appropriated every generator in the region."

"Appropriated? You mean you stole them," Ferret said.

"No. Some of them weren't in use when we found them. As for those that were," the officer said, smirking, "let us say the owners were quite happy to part with their generators instead of their lives. Quite an even trade in my estimation."

Ferret spied an enormous pit several dozen yards to the east. "What's with the big hole?"

"The Baron is quite a collector. In that pit are seventeen of the largest alligators in the entire bayou."

"Are they his pets?"

"He uses them for disciplinary purposes."

"I'll bet he doesn't have many discipline problems."

Captain François glanced over his shoulder and grinned. "You are very astute."

"If I were astute I wouldn't be here."

They followed a winding cement walk across the huge lawn fronting the mansion. Grand old cypress and oak trees dotted the meticulously tended capret of green grass, and artistically arranged flower gardens lent a touch of elegance to the den of iniquity.

Ferret stared at the mansion. Earlier, when the *tonton macoutes* had escorted them from the pier to the prison tower, they had hiked along the base of the south wall directly to their cell without much opportunity to study the estate. Now he noticed a row of cages on each side of the portico and heard growls and hissing noises. "What are those?" he asked.

"The Baron's prized collection of relatives of yours," Captain François said, and snickered. "Beastly mutations."

Ferret and Gremlin looked at one another.

"The Baron has been collecting for over a decade," François related. "Every hunter and trapper in the bayou knows they will receive a hefty reward if they bring in the kind of creatures the Baron likes."

The animal sounds grew in volume as their party neared the mansion.

Various scents were borne to Ferret's sensitive nose by

the cool night breeze: bear, bobcat, raccoon, deer, and others. Overriding them all was the tangy odor of primal fear. Ferret felt a strong sympathy for the creatures being confined.

Six *tonton macoutes* were posted as guards outside the front door, three on each side, and all six promptly snapped to attention when that door unexpectedly opened and out strolled a man and a woman.

Ferret sensed a change in the officer and the men in black serving as the escort, a subtle tensing of their bodies, a barely concealed air of sheer dread. Such a reaction convinced him the pair on the portico must be the Baron and Majesta, and he studied them with interest.

Majesta was a woman in her thirties, possessed of a full figure, long black hair, and features akin to chiseled marble. She wore an unusual green dress that scarcely covered her jutting breasts, the shape of the fabric resembling the twisted coils of a snake.

The Baron wore all red. His hawkish, cruel visage perfectly fit the man. Dark, malevolent eyes regarded the approaching party without a hint of friendly emotion. From his right hip, suspended in an ornate sheath, hung a dagger with a bejeweled golden hilt. "So these are the genetic deviates," he declared by way of a greeting.

"You're not exactly the cream of the crop yourself, sucker," Ferret responded, and instantly regretted his rash impulse when a man in black spun and clubbed him on the right temple. He staggered but stayed erect.

"Leave him alone, yes!" Gremlin spoke up.

"Neither of you will talk unless addressed," the Baron informed them imperiously. He came down the steps slowly, examining the prisoners intently. "Amazing. Truly amazing. You're the first mutations I've seen who are so closely similar to man."

"They not only have the power of speech, your lordship," Captain François stated with a slight bow, "but they can also operate firearms."

"Really?" the Baron responded. "If we're not careful,

one day these deviates will rise up against us and try to take over."

Ferret had taken all the insults he could tolerate. "Who are you calling a deviate, you misfit? We're half human, and we—"

A stocky *tonton macoute*, at a curt nod from the Baron, began beating the hybrid on the head with a vengeance.

Ferret tried to raise his hands to protect his face, but another man in black struck him in the small of the back, causing him to fall to his knees.

"No!" Gremlin cried, stepping to his friend's aid. He stepped between the stocky assailant and Ferret, using his own body as a shield.

"Enough!" the Baron commanded, and grinned. "How touching. They claim to be part human and demonstrate brotherly loyalty. But in the final analysis they are still genetic aberrations. These two are quite unique, but they would pose too many problems if I added them to my menagerie. You were right in your estimation, my dear captain, but I had to see for myself." He paused and glanced at the woman. "What do you think, Majesta?"

"Damballah would enjoy them."

"My thoughts exactly. They would be delightful appetizers," the Baron said, and faced the officer. "Very well. Take them back to their cell. It's ten-thirty now. In forty minutes bring them here so they can join our procession to the *houmfor*. We must be on time and commence the ceremony at midnight."

"As you wish, my lordship," Captain François said.

Ferret heard the words through a veil of pain. He grimaced and managed to straighten with Gremlin's assistance. Footsteps pounded on the walk to their rear and another man in black raced past them to halt in front of the Baron.

"What is it?" the head of the Black Society demanded brusquely.

"Forgive this intrusion, Great One," the man stated, and bent at the waist. "A speedboat has just arrived from New

Orleans.''

The Baron frowned. ''I gave specific orders that the speed-boat is only to be employed on special occasions. It uses too much of our precious fuel to be utilized without proper justification. Who has committed this oversight?''

''Sergeant Valmy, sir. He sent me on ahead to tell you the news and explain his reason.''

''This had better be good.''

''The sergeant has captured another mutation like these two, your lordship.''

''What?'' the Baron exclaimed.

''Yes, sir. He was on routine patrol along the shore of the bayou. The creature he has captured is a cat of some kind. He also has a woman with him, and he suspects she is a member of the Resistance.''

''Does this woman have a name?''

''Sergeant Valvy told me she was unconscious when he found her, but she has been revived and persuaded to talk. Eleanore DeCoud is her name, great one.''

The Baron placed his hands on his hips and laughed uproariously, then twisted to stare at Majesta. ''All things come to those who worship Damballah.''

''Indeed,'' the *mambo* said, smirking wickedly. ''The Snake God will feast well tonight.''

CHAPTER
EIGHTEEN

The *tonton macoutes* spotted him.

Blade had only one option. Retreating into the undergrowth where the snappers lurked was out of the question. Trying to outrun the boat along the shoreline couldn't be done. Since the enemy had seen him and now voiced loud shouts while slanting their boat in his direction, he decided to use the time-tested strategy advocated by skilled fighters down through the centuries.

The best defense is always a good offense.

The Warrior raced the ten feet to the edge of the bayou and dived into the water, his huge form cleaving the surface smoothly. He found the depth to be a mere five feet and quickly made for the deeper area farther out.

From the south came the distinctive buzzing drone of the boat's outboard.

Blade stayed close to the bottom, sweeping strands of underwater vegetation aside with his forearms. He gazed upward, gauging the depth, pleased when it increased to ten feet, then 15.

The underside of the craft appeared, moving quite slowly,

and the heads and shoulders of several men in black were visible although distorted by the water. They were standing in the boat and peering into the bayou.

Would they see him? Blade wondered, holding steady, his hands moving back and forth. He placed his feet on the bottom, testing to determine its sponginess. Once assured that his legs wouldn't sink in the mud, he crouched and waited for the right moment.

The craft weaved slightly from side to side, coming ever closer.

Blade watched the boat creep almost directly overhead, its motor making a put-put noise, and he launched himself at the underside like a human missile, is arms sweeping up and out, hoping the element of surprise would enable him to overcome his six armed foes.

The boat was barely moving.

Kicking powerfully, the Warrior swam for the starboard side. He girded himself to act swiftly, decisively, and he was ready when his arms broke the surface right next to the craft. In that very instant he gripped the upper edge and hauled downward, counting on the fact that all the *tonton macoutes* were standing to unbalance their boat and possibly tip it over.

The strategy succeeded.

Caught totally off guard, the voodoo cult members on the port side were thrown against those on the starboard, and together their combined weight served to tip the boat at an almost verticle angle and dump all of them into the swamp.

Blade had already released the top when the first man in black hit the water. The rest followed suit in a confused mass, and he whipped the Bowies from their sheaths and tore into them, taking advantage of their momentary disorientation as they went under. Their first reaction was to thrash and make for the surface again, leaving them vulnerable to his attack.

Arcing to the left, Blade buried both knives in the chest of the first man under, then wrenched them out and turned, going for three foes at once, his movement impeded by the water but still forceful enough for him to slash one *tonton macoute* across the throat and stab the other pair.

Leaving just two.

The Warrior twisted and saw the remaining duo trying to clamber onto the stalled boat. He came at them from below, spearing his right Bowie into the unprotected abdomen of the nearest man in black, ripping the stomach wide open, and then attacked his final adversary.

Displaying remarkable agility, the last *tonton macoute*, who was dangling over the starboard side, flipped his legs up and rolled into the craft. In another moment he reappeared at the side, an M1 carbine pressed to his right shoulder.

Blade was a mere six feet from the side of the boat. He abruptly bent at the waist and shot toward the underside, and his head passed underneath the bottom just as the *tonton macoute* cut loose. The blasting of the M1 was muted but audible. He bent in half again to draw his legs out of sight that much faster, expecting to feel a stinging sensation at any second.

The firing suddenly stopped.

The Warrior's lungs were beginning to ache. He couldn't stay under that much longer. His exertions had used up too much precious oxygen. He figured the man in black must be waiting for him to poke his head out, but he had another idea. Sinking down about a yard, he swam straight up and rammed his right shoulder into the middle of the boat, which rocked and swayed from the impact. Again he repeated the maneuver, and yet once more, and after the third hit he swam to the right and broke the surface right next to the bobbing craft while sliding the left Bowie into its sheath.

Upright in the center of the boat, the *tonton macoute* struggled to retain his footing despite the rolling motion. His wide eyes probed the gloomy depths for the giant, focused on the spot where he had last seen him.

Surging out of the water, Blade used his left hand on the top of the side to propel himself from the opposite direction, his arm extended, the Bowie straight out.

The man in black spun.

Too late.

The Bowie caught the *tonton macoute* in the groin, and
he screeched and doubled over, the M1 clattering at his feet.

With only the upper half of his torso in the boat, Blade
had to rely strictly on his massive arms. As always, his
rippling sinews were equal to the occasion. He let go of the
side, reached out to grab his foe's black shirt, and pulled
the man toward him. Jerking the knife free, he lanced the
bloody tip into the man's chest above the heart. Twice he
stabbed, and his adversary abruptly wheezed and went limp.

Blade allowed the *tonton macoute* to drop, then climbed
all the way into the craft and paused to catch his breath. He
saw several bodies floating to the east, and one man kicked
feebly in water stained crimson to the south.

Something else moved to the south.

A 15-foot alligator, only its head and back visible, bore
down on the bodies with startling speed.

The Warrior scooped up the M1 and stood, ready in case
the reptile should attempt to come after him. But his concern
turned out to be groundless.

Never slowing, the gator swam straight at the lone *tonton
macoute* who still struggled, however weakly, its tail creating
a wake for yards to its rear.

Blade simply watched, unwilling to intervene. He saw the
alligator open its mouth at the very last instant and take the
man into its teeth-filled maw. Immediately the reptile began
rolling over and over, twirling the body end over end.

The *tonton macoute* uttered a pathetic, gurgling scream.

As if on that cue, the gator abruptly dived, taking its supper
along. A flurry of bubbles marked the spot for half a minute,
then subsided.

The Warrior had seen enough. Every second he delayed
increased the likelihood of other men in black showing up
if they'd heard the gunfire. He stooped, took hold of the last
one he had killed, and hurled the man into the bayou.
Rotating and kneeling, he worked on the outboard for a few
seconds, and was rewarded by the motor roaring to life.

Taking a seat and laying the M1 in front of him, he steered a course due north, having decided to swing in a wipe loop to evade other boats that might be looking for him.

The encroaching night rapidly reduced the field of vision.

Blade proceeded slowly, wary of striking a submerged log or some other obstruction. He realized the *tonton macoutes* must have a means of navigating at night and he checked the bottom of the boat. Under the middle seat he discovered a watertight wooden box secured by a small clasp. Opening it, he found a half-dozen tools apparently intended for use should the motor give out and a small portable spotlight that could be clamped to the side of the craft and swiveled in any given direction.

But would it work?

The Warrior attached the spotlight to his right and flicked the black switch on the top. A bright beam illuminated the swamp ahead for a distance of 20 yards. His brow creased as he pondered the implications. The spotlight operated on battery power, which meant the Black Snake Society either possessed a supply of new batteries they had obtained from an unknown source, perhaps from the Russian zone through the black market, or else they owned generators and a stockpile of rechargeable batteries. Both possibilities indicated the organization was efficiently, if cruelly, operated.

Blade settled back for the ride, unsure of the amount of time it would take him to reach the stronghold. Even with the aid of the spotlight, he would have to proceed relatively slowly. Underwater obstacles could still pose a problem. One hole in the bottom and he'd face the distinctly unpleasant chore of swimming all the way there.

A bayou at night was not the most hospitable of environments.

As the minutes dragged by the light revealed the nocturnal wildlife on the prowl: huge alligators cruising about seeking a meal, snakes of varying proportions moving their sleek forms in the telltale wavy pattern, enormous bullfrogs searching for insects, and big bugs looking for little bugs. Where only a handful of each species had been abroad during the daylight hours, after dark the water teemed with creatures, primarily predators.

Blade was particularly impressed by the number of snakes.

Once, off to the west, a tremendous splashing occurred, as if a gargantuan animal were throwing a temper tantrum in the water, and the sound persisted for over three minutes.

The Warrior stared intently, striving to ascertain the source. He switched off the spotlight, concerned the thing might be attracted to it. His first thoughts were of Damballah. If the snake should come after him, the M1 might not stop such a massive reptile. When the sound stopped he waited another minute before turning on the light again. Keenly alert, he proceeded north about a mile and a half, very slowly, then doubled back.

After an interval that seemed like hours he spotted pinpoints of luminosity far ahead. If his mental calculations were correct, he was approaching the island from the northwest. So the lights he saw couldn't be located in the vicinity of the compound, which occupied the southern end, because they were much farther north than they should be and there were only a few. The Baron's fortress would be ablaze with illumination.

Then what could this be?

Blade killed his own spotlight and slanted the boat toward the mysterious lights. In another hundred yards he came to the conclusion they were situated at the north end of the Baron's island.

A guard post maybe?

Cautiously now, the Warrior guided the craft ever nearer until he could distinguish the shapes of trees lining the north shore. Fifty yards from the trees stood a two-story structure, and the lights he saw were situated near it.

A guard post wouldn't be two stories high.

Puzzled, Blade shut off the outboard and let the boat drift toward the island. He lifted the M1 and moved to the bow, his eyes gradually adjusting to the darkness. The shore appeared abruptly and the bottom of the craft rubbed on the waterlogged earth underneath.

Now!

Blade vaulted from the boat, the water only rising to his ankles, and ran nimbly to solid ground. He crouched, fingering the trigger, scanning the landscape. The vegetation under the trees presented a formidable inky wall to his probing eyes, but 15 yards to the left a wide path or road ran straight from the bayou in the direction of the structure.

The *tonton macoutes* must come here frequently.

He ran to the path, which turned out to be a flattened track of grass ten feet in width, then jogged toward the building. All around him insects strummed and buzzed.

Someone laughed.

The faint titter stopped Blade in his tracks and he flattened. It came from the structure. After ten seconds he rose, staying bent over, and moved forward. Indistinct voices reached his ears.

The lights solidified as lanterns hanging from hooks positioned at 40-foot intervals on the outside of the circular structure. The walls were made of polished wood. Between each lantern was an arched opening.

Blade edged toward one of the entrances, perplexed by the shape of the building. It resembled a stadium more than anything else, and for the life of him he couldn't comprehend why a stadium would be located way out in the middle of the tropical growth proliferating on the north side of the island. Why not simply construct the edifice near the compound? There must be a reason.

The voices grew louder, almost audible.

Exercising the utmost care, the giant stepped to the arch and peered within. A short tunnel led to an inner open area. He was about to advance when he noticed another arched doorway off to the right, only this one was twice the size of all the others, a virtual tunnel.

Strange.

Blade crept along the right-hand wall until he was within three feet of the inner arch, then halted. Now he could hear the voices clearly.

"—don't know why we have to sweep this out every time. It's not like it matters."

"Brother, you'd best not let the Baron or Majesta hear you talking like that or you'll find yourself in the same boat as those poor freaks."

"Listen to who's talking! You know how the Baron hates them things. If he thought for a minute that you felt sorry for the critters, your ass would be grass."

"Don't I know it."

Blade inched to the edge and risked a look. His surprised gaze alighted on a pair of *tonton macoutes*, one white and the other black, who were sweeping the spacious open area comprising the middle two thirds of the circular structure. What surprised him the most was the fact they were using brooms on a *dirt floor*.

"How much time we got?" asked the white one.

The black consulted a watch on his left wrist. "Let's see. The procession won't leave the compound until eleven-fifteen, and it'll take them a half hour to get here. So we've got about an hour to kill."

"I wish Captain François had picked somebody else for this damn detail," stated the first man, glancing nervously at the west side of the arena.

Blade did the same, his eyes narrowing at the sight of six posts imbedded in the ground near the smooth inner wall, each spaced approximately ten feet apart. Affixed to every post was a set of shackles, and he could readily imagine the function they would serve. He gazed upward and discovered another interesting aspect to the structure.

The smooth arena wall only extended for a height of 15 feet. Above it were rows of tightly packed bleachers for an audience of a hundred or more. There was no roof, only stars.

All of a sudden the pieces of the puzzle fit.

Blade was about to draw back from the archway when he glanced to the east and spied the great drum occupying a spot all by itself at the front of the bleachers. He remembered the words of Henry Pétion and scowled.

How could he hope to do it?

Do the impossible?

Defeat Damballah?

The Warrior melted into the shadows. He had an hour in which to devise a brilliant strategy, or in an hour and a half he would likely be dead.

CHAPTER NINETEEN

Lynx was not a happy hybrid.

He considered being captured as a personal affront to his dignity and his mutant prowess. To make matters worse, the jerk heading the detail responsible for his capture had taunted him all the way from New Orleans to the Baron's estate, calling him every name in the book. The slimeball had also refused to give Eleanore any food—just water. That alone had revived her, but she had been so weak the *tonton macoutes* were compelled to carry her from the speedboat when it docked at the island.

What was the name of that SOB again? Lynx asked himself. Oh, yeah. Sergeant Valmy. If he ever got his nails into the good sergeant, Valmy would look like shredded venison. That was a promise.

Poor Eleanore.

Lynx wished they had been placed in the same cell. Instead, they had been taken directly from the pier to a prison tower and he'd been shoved into a room all by his lonesome, his arms bound with nylon cord.

Valmy had suspected he would give them a hassle.

The bozo didn't know the half of it.

And now, after tearing the cord off with his teeth and pacing the cell for at least 30 minutes, Lynx was becoming increasingly impatient. He'd tried the window and the door repeatedly, but both were proof against even his prodigious strength.

Damn it all.

A few second later, when he detected the sound of someone approaching his cell door, he snickered and dashed to the right, standing next to the jamb. When the door swung outward, he'd leap on the bastards before they knew what hit them. He heard the bolt sliding free, and tensed.

"I know you can hear me in there," declared someone through the thin slot. "Stand in the open where I can see you and do it now."

Lynx stayed where he was out of sheer spite.

"Listen to me, mutation. My name is Captain François. I have no time for games. Your friends are already waiting for you outside, as is the woman you were brought here with. Unless you want them to be harmed, you will do exactly as I say."

They had him over a barrel, Lynx realized, and he stepped to the middle of the cell, his shoulders slumped in resignation. "How's this, turkey?"

Dark eyes regarded the hybrid critically. "I was told you were bound."

"Yeah. I was, but the cord just slipped right off. I guess they don't make nylon like they used to, huh?"

"Raise your arms," Captain François directed.

"Okay. But I warn you. I didn't take my shower today."

The door was jerked wide and two *tonton macoutes* entered briskly, submachine guns clutched in their hands. After them came the officer.

"Sergeant Valmy told me your name is Lynx," François said.

"I didn't think the dodo could remember his own name, let alone mine."

François clasped his hands behind his back. "You would be well advised to keep that smart mouth of yours in check. It can only get you into trouble."

"What would you call this?"

The captain barely suppressed a grin, then spoke over his left shoulder. "Get in here and bind him."

Another pair of men in black walked into the cell and swiftly coiled loops of nylon around the hybrid's wrists, using three times as much cord as before.

"Are you sure this is enough?" Lynx quipped.

"Let's go," Captain François stated, and gestured at the doorway.

"Where are you takin' me?" Lynx asked as he walked out.

"For a little stroll in the fresh air."

Six more *tonton macoutes* were waiting in the corridor.

"All this just for me?" Lynx said, baiting them. "I'm flattered."

"Not just for you," Captain François said, correcting him. "For the others too."

"How are my three pals doing, anyway?"

"One of them has escaped."

Lynx beamed at the news. "Let me guess. The big guy with muscles growin' out of his muscles."

"How did you know?"

"The other two couldn't escape from a soggy paper bag."

Captain François led the escort down the metal stairway to the bottom floor.

The prospect of seeing his friends again filled Lynx with joy. He could barely contain himself as the outer door was opened and he was ushered outside. And there they stood, covered by four *tonton macoutes:* Ferret, Gremlin, and Eleanore DeCoud.

"Lynx!" Gremlin exclaimed happily, and wagged his bound arms. "Are you okay, yes?"

"I'm fine," Lynx responded. He grinned and sauntered over to them. Oddly, Ferret avoided meeting his gaze. "What about you guys?"

"We weren't harmed, no," Gremlin said.

"Speak for yourself," Ferret muttered, studiously staring off into the distance.

"What happened?" Lynx asked.

"You tell him," Ferret instructed the humanoid.

"Poor Ferret was beat on by these fiends, yes."

"Are you all right?" Lynx inquired of his fellow hybrid.

Again Ferret addressed Gremlin. "Would you tell this—person—that I'm alive, no thanks to him."

Lynx glanced at the humanoid, who shrugged, then at Ferret. "What's going on here? Aren't you talking to me?"

"No."

"Why not?"

"I don't have a year to go into the reasons."

"Oh. Is that right? I'm beginning to think you're a bit ticked off at me."

"*A bit?*" Ferret unexpectedly exploded, and before anyone could guess his intent, before any of the *tonton macoutes* could intervene, before Gremlin could stop him, he sprang forward, sweeping his arms up and out. Despite the cord binding his wrists he managed to open his hands wide enough to clamp his fingers on the cat-man's throat.

"Ferret! No, no!" Gremlin cried.

"What the hell!" Captain François blurted out in amazement.

The best Lynx could do was grab his friend's arm and utter a sound that came out as "Gaaaacck!"

To Ferret, the few seconds he had his hands on the cat-man's neck were sheer rapture. He didn't actually squeeze hard enough to do any harm, but the simple sensation of applying enough pressure to cause Lynx to cough and sputter, and beholding the inanely stupid expression on his chronic tormentor, produced a profound ecstasy.

"Pull them apart!" Captain François barked.

Two men in black shouldered their weapons and moved in, one tugging on Lynx while the other attempted to pry Ferret's hands off. When this second man realized the mutations's diminutive size belied the steely strength resident in the hybrid's slim limbs, he called out for help.

Lynx wheezed and thrashed, frantically striving to pull free.

Three more *tonton macoutes* rushed to the assistance of their comrades, and between the four of them they were finally able to tear Ferret's hands loose.

"What's the meaning of this?" Captain François demanded angrily. "I thought the two of you were friends."

Inhaling raggedly, Lynx glanced at the officer and tried to speak. His throat hurt like hell and he had to lick his lips and wet his mouth before he succeeded. "So did I," he croaked.

Ferret, held fast by four men in black, startled everyone by throwing back his head and cackling uproariously, uncontrollably venting the emotional release he needed, laughing in supreme delight.

"The freak is crazy, sir," one of the *tonton macoutes* commented.

"You may be right," François concurred.

Lynx glanced at Gremlin, stunned to find the humanoid snickering, then at Ferret. "What was that all about, you idiot! You almost killed me!"

Ferret only laughed louder.

"I don't see what's so damn funny," Lynx snapped, completely confused.

"Neither do I," Captain François declared. "I don't know what's going on here, but I do know we will not have a repeat of this performance or the offender will suffer the painful consequence." He paused and stared at the man restraining Ferret. "Let him go."

The quartet promptly obeyed.

"Since you obviously can't be trusted together," François went on, "I'm going to have two of my men walk between each of you. There will be no talking whatsoever. Understood?"

"Where are we going?" Lynx inquired.

"For a little stroll," François said, and swept his men with a stern stare. "All right. Fall in."

Lynx stepped over to Eleanore, who had witnessed the incident in stunned silence, and noticed her eyes were drooping. "Hey, sweetcheeks. How are you holdin' up?"

"Okay," she replied weakly. "I could use some sleep, though."

"Have they fed you yet?"

"No."

The cat-man turned toward the officer. "Before we go anywhere, why don't you feed the babe?"

"That's not possible," Captain François answered.

"Sure it is, dimwit. Just go over to the fancy house over there and ask the kitchen help for some leftovers."

"Your insolence is becoming annoying, freak. When I said feeding her isn't possible, I meant it. Besides, food is the least of her worries."

"What's that supposed to mean?"

"Never mind. And now you'll shut your furry face or we'll kick your teeth in."

Furious, Lynx opened his mouth, then thought better of the notion. His intuition told him he'd need to be in tiptop shape to handle whatever the tutti-fruittis threw at him. Reluctantly, he held his temper in check and smiled reassuringly at Eleanore.

She feebly returned the smile.

The *tonton macoutes* arranged themselves as the captain had stipulated, separating the hybrids and the woman from each other. At a word from François the detail headed for the mansion with him in the lead.

Lynx hiked behind two men in black, sullenly plotting to disembowel every last *tonton macoute* on the planet. He was extremely concerned about the woman. She needed food and rest badly, and there had to be a way he could get her both. Preoccupied with his musing, he failed to pay special attention to the mansion until they were within 30 yards of the portico. Then he glanced up in consternation at the subdued murmur of many voices to discover over four dozen men in black standing in formation, at ease, on the lawn near the front door.

Look at them all!

Where had they all come from? Lynx wondered. He hadn't seen anywhere near that many when he'd arrived at the compound. A glance over his left shoulder at the gate in the south wall showed him more *tonton macoutes* hurrying in from the pier. He also glimpsed 25 or 30 boats tied at dock.

The dorks must be arriving from all over.

Which did not bode well.

Lynx frowned and gazed at the mansion. They wouldn't be calling in all the troops unless the activity planned for the night was very special. What did black-magic types do for kicks anyway?

The murmur of conversation abruptly ceased when the door opened and out strode a man dressed in red and a woman wearing a green dress. Instantly the *tonton macoutes* snapped to attention.

Captain François led his detail straight up to the steps and bowed. "Here are the prisoners, your lordship," he announced.

"The Baron and Majesta," Eleanore stated in evident horror, raising the back of her left hand to her mouth.

Smirking wickedly, the man called the Baron came down and stood next to the officer. The malevolent gaze fastened onto Eleanore. "Well, well, well. It's been a while, hasn't it, Ms. DeCoud?"

"You bastard!"

The Baron chuckled and looked up at the woman in green. "Look who's here, Majesta. Our old friend Eleanore."

"Hello, Eleanore," the *mambo* said sweetly.

"Screw you."

"It appears she's developed an attitude problem," Majesta remarked sarcastically.

"Poor Eleanore always was an independent thinker," the Baron mentioned. "Perhaps that's why she saw fit to join the Resistance after her stay here was over."

"You don't have any proof," Eleanore declared, taking a step toward him.

"What's that?"

"You don't have any proof I joined the Resistance. You're just guessing," Eleanore reiterated.

The Baron grinned smugly. "First of all, what makes you think I need proof? If I believe someone is guilty of conspiring against the Black Snake Society, then they're guilty." He paused. "However, in your case I do happen to have concrete substantiation of your betrayal."

"Liar."

"Oh?" The Baron twisted, looking at the entrance. "Would you come out now, my dear," he called out.

Another woman emerged from the mansion. She wore a blue dress styled to accent her feminine charms. Her blond hair bobbed as she walked, and her green eyes regarded the captives coldly, especially one of them.

Lynx saw Eleanore's eyes widen and heard her gasp. She swayed, about to fall, but recovered and cried shrilly, "Violet!"

"Litte Eleanore," Violet said, her tone reeking with disdain. "At long last you're about to get your just desserts."

"You've turned against the Resistance," Eleanore declared in disbelief.

"You fool. I've never been *with* the Resistance," Violet replied.

"But you're the leader of the movement!"

"What movement? A few pathetic fools foolishly attempting to overthrow the Black Snake Society? Don't make me laugh."

"This can't be happening."

"But it is, you dumb bitch. I've been one of the Baron's favorites ever since he first brought me here when I was fifteen. Unlike you, I knew a good thing when I saw it. I agreed to work with him, to do whatever he wanted, and he instructed me to infiltrate the Resistance. Neither of us ever imagined I'd become the leader."

"But why?" Eleanore asked, her voice wavering.

"Are you that dumb you can't figure it out? What better way to keep tabs on the opposition than to have someone on the inside? I keep him informed of all Resistance activities. I provide him with the names of all Resistance members."

"Why not just wipe it out?"

"Because new malcontents are bound to arise, and this way the Black Snake Society keeps track of each and every one. Why wipe the Resistance out when we control those opposed to us?"

Eleanore appeared dazed by the revelations. "I still don't understand. What about the radio?"

"What about it? I sabotaged the shortwave. Even if someone had heard Adrien's weak signal, they would never have been able to get through. We let him go on broadcasting for a couple of weeks to ensure any suspicion that arose after he was captured would be diverted from me," Violet boasted.

"Enough of this," the Baron suddenly snapped. "The bitch doesn't deserve to know all of our secrets." He faced the assembled *tonton macoutes*. "Tonight is a special night, my brothers. Tonight we offer our living god the sacrifices Damballah requires to continue bestowing on us the power that makes us invincible. Tonight we show Damballah the depths of our devotion. We will renew our covenant with the Divine Serpent, and in return our magic will become even stronger than it already is. Are you ready to recommit yourselves?"

Responding on cue, as if they had done this many times previously, the *tonton macoutes* shouted as one: "Yes, we are!"

"Excellent. Then let us proceed."

Lynx barely paid attention as Majesta and Violet joined the twit in red, orders were barked, lanterns brought, and the entire procession walked northward, skirting the mansion. He was too concerned about Eleanore. She walked in a trancelike state, shuffling lethargically, apparently in shock over discovering the truth about Violet. Which reminded him. He added the blonde to the list of scuzzbuckets he intended to waste before he departed New Orleans.

After rounding the mansion the Black Snake Society marched due north to another gate in the outer walls. The iron barrier was promptly opened, and walking with his head high and his shoulders squared, in the manner of a king of old, Baron Laveau led his followers along a clear-cut path, continuing to the north.

Lynx resigned himself to going along with the program for the time being. More *tonton macoutes* had surrounded him as they started out, and at least ten weapons were trained on him at all times. If he so much as sneezed they might blow him away. He noted that Ferret and Gremlin were receiving similar treatment.

The path bore on a generally direct course toward the far side of the island. Thick vegetation and tall trees flanked both sides. An unnatural stillness pervaded the forest. Even the insects had fallen silent at the passage of so many humans.

Since he had nothing better to do, and since the lanterns weren't bright enough to dispel all of the shadows, particularly from the waist down, Lynx availed himself of the opportunity to work on the cords securing his wrists. The last time he'd used his teeth. This time he had to strain against the nylon, then relax, and repeat the procedure over and over in the hope the cord would slacken.

The trek seemed endless.

Just when Lynx was about to ask if the dummies knew where they were going, a two-story structure appeared ahead. It was ringed by torches, and there were arched entranceways all along the base. He didn't like the looks of it.

The Baron halted before one of the entrances and motioned with his right arm.

With the practiced precision acquired by previous experience, the *tonton macoutes* closed on their prisoners.

Lynx was caught off guard. A dozen men in black swarmed all over him, seizing his arms and legs and hoisting him into the air. He struggled in vain, unable to utilize his nails, hissing like his namesake. He felt the men move, and in less than a minute he had been carried through a dark tunnel and into an enormous arena. A smooth wall enclosed the open area to a height of 15 feet, then there were bleachers.

Somewhere nearby, Ferret was snarling in frustrated rage.

The *tonton macoutes* abruptly lowered Lynx to the ground, holding him tightly. A hard object brushed against his back. Then his captors astonished him; they sliced the nylon cords from his wrists. Elated, he flexed his fingers. But the next moment his elation changed to feral wrath when the cords were replaced by metal shackles. "No!" he bellowed, and heaved.

The men in black had already started to release him. They hastened off toward one of the openings, snickering and laughing.

Lynx looked behind him to discover a wooden post to which the shackles were fastened. Four feet of chain afforded limited mobility. A hasty glance to his right revealed Ferret and Gremlin chained to other posts. To his left was Eleanore, sagging lifelessly with her eyes closed.

"The best is yet to come, freak."

The mocking voice drew Lynx's gaze upward to the bleachers.

Seated above the posts and leaning over the edge was the Baron. "Are you ready for the main event? It's almost midnight."

"What happens? Do you turn into a pumpkin?"

"Not quite," Baron Laveau said, and nodded at the opposite side of the arena.

Lynx glanced in that direction and spotted a huge drum. "Let me guess. You're having a dance?"

"Of a sort," the Baron replied, grinning. "A dance of death."

The *tonton macoutes* were almost all in position for the ceremony, dutifully filling the bleachers from bottom to top, walking up narrow aisles to reach the higher rows.

Lynx tested the shackles, surging against the steel chains, and fumed when they proved to be more than a match for his genetically heightened strength. He recalled several stories he'd heard to the effect that Blade had broken chains on one or two occasions, and doubted whether even the giant could break those restraining him. But he had to find a way to get loose. If he didn't—

"Let the ceremony begin!" Baron Laveau shouted, standing. He beamed at Majesta and Violet, who were on his left, and then glanced toward the drum. "Sound the Sacred Drum."

Lynx saw a tall man lift a mallet of some sort and strike the drum. The booming retort reverberated in the arena and wafted out over the bayou. He guessed the sound could be heard for miles under the right conditions.

The *tonton macoutes* began to chant in an unknown language.

Again the mallet struck the drum, and again the thunderous percussion echoed on the night breeze.

Lynx suspected what was coming. He ignored the drumming and the chanting of the *tonton macoutes,* who had only filled slightly over half the bleachers, and devoted his energy to breaking the chains. He wrenched and pulled and jerked in reckless abandon, heedless of the pain the shackles caused as they dug into his wrists. If he didn't get free, he was dead. And he didn't want to die. Not when Melody was waiting anxiously for his return. Not when he had so much to live for. A future with the woman he loved. Young ones, kids of his very own.

Damn the injustice of it all!

His arms hurting terribly, his wrists bleeding profusely, Lynx kept at his task with undiminished intensity. His hybrid stamina enabled him to persist far beyond the point where a human would have weakened and collapsed. He bared his fangs, his chest heaving, and struggled, struggled, struggled. The drumming had become a monotonous backdrop to his efforts, the chanting a litany goading him to continually

renew his attempts. Only when he heard Ferret yelling his
name did he finally cease and stay still, weary to his core,
dripping sweat and blood. He looked to his right.

"Don't you see it?" Ferret asked in consternation.

"Dear God, no!" Gremlin declared.

Lynx shifted, and every hair on his neck and shoulders
stood on end at the horrifying apparition slithering from a
tunnel not 50 feet away. He inadvertently gasped and
recoiled.

Damballah had arrived.

The Snake God of the bayou.

Primal power incarnate.

Lynx's worst nightmare. He crouched and formed his
fingers into rigid claws, growling fiercely, resolved to go
out fighting to the last. Fear tried to dominate him, sparked
by his dread of all snakes, and he asserted self-control with
a supreme exertion of willpower.

The drumming stopped. The chanting too. An expectant,
heavy hush descended on the area. The gathered members
of the Black Snake Society gaped at their Deity.

Damballah entered the temple slowly. The monstrous
reptile drew its entire 40-foot length inside, then slid toward
the posts as it had done countless times in the past, its chilling
orbs fixed on the creatures it would soon devour.

Lynx had never felt so helpless. The titanic serpent dwarfed
him into insignificance; he'd be swallowed in one gulp.

"Oh great Damballah!" Baron Laveau called out. "Hear
our prayer. Accept these tokens for our loyalty and grant us
continued good fortune! Take them! They are yours."

The Snake God crossed to within six feet of the sacrificial
posts and halted. Its mighty head rose into the air. Ten feet.
Twelve.

Lynx saw the thing looking at him, and trembled.

"Feast on these morsels!" the Baron yelled. "Enjoy the
fruits of our labor for you!"

Damballah's head rose ponderously, the great reptile
staring at the man in red.

Lynx also glanced upward, wishing he could throttle the Baron's neck, peeved at the idea of being killed without a chance of retribution, and because he was the only person in the whole temple to be gazing in that direction, because everyone else had eyes only for the snake, he alone saw it, he alone witnessed the giant rising from concealment behind the bleachers at the very top, he alone observed the herculean seven-foot-tall figure race down the aisle to the right of the Baron, he alone saw the cyclopean makeshift spear clenched in the giant's brawny hands, a spear ten feet in length and six inches in diameter, fashioned from the limb of an oak tree and sharpened to a point by the Bowies the giant always wore.

Blade was there!

Tensing in anticipation, Lynx watched as Blade came to the end of the aisle near the Baron. He expected the giant to hurl the spear. Instead, in awe and wonderment, he saw Blade place a combat boot on the very edge and vault into the air, leaping high and wide.

The giant's momentum and bulging muscles served him in good stead. He arced up and over Damballah's head, and at the apex of his leap, at the very instant he hung in the air over the serpent's eyes, he bent in half and swung the spear with all the force in his arms and shoulders, driving the point into the snake's flesh, penetrating to half the length of the spear, and held on tight.

For a heartbeat nothing happened.

Suddenly the Snake God exploded into action. Damballah's mouth opened wide and it hissed louder than a thousand cottonmouths. Its body convulsed, and its head shot even higher and thrashed wildly.

Blade clung to the spear in desperation, his arms and legs wrapped around the shaft.

Majesta screamed.

The black snake rose almost 20 feet, half of its span suspended above the posts, and then it crashed down, falling between Lynx and Ferret, a full third of its body smashing over the rim and onto the bleachers, onto the Baron and the women with him, crushing them.

Blade let go of the spear and jumped. He landed to the right of the serpent, took hold of the top of the smooth wall, and swung down to the arena.

Above him pandemonium erupted. Damballah continued to convulse in a violent paroxysm of monumental proportions, bearing to the left on the bleachers, sliding over *tonton macoutes* or battering them aside with its blunt head. Screeches of anguish and terror filled the temple. Panic spread like wildfire, and those men in black who could do so, fled. But the majority never made it out. Limp, broken bodies lay everywhere. Damballah slid onward, making a mindless curcuit of the arena, moving slower and slower. In less than a minute the Snake God devastated those who worshipped it, and the destruction didn't stop until Damballah plowed into the Sacred Drum and sounded the resounding beat for the final time. The serpent sagged, its head jutting from the ruptured skin, and expired.

Blade ran to the posts and stopped next to the cat-man. "This is the last time I bring you guys on a mission," he stated.

Staggered by the snake's demise, by the havoc, by his own close call, Lynx looked at the giant in confusion. "What? What did you say?"

"I'm not bringing you bozos on another run."

"Why not?" Lynx asked absently, gazing at Damballah.

A grin creased the giant's mouth. "Because here I am doing all the work while you three just hang around."

"Has anyone ever told you that you have a *pitiful* sense of humor?"

EPILOGUE

"So what the hell are we doing back here?" Lynx snapped, squinting up at the noon sun.

"Unfinished business," Blade said.

"Gremlin thought we had everything wrapped up, yes?" the humanoid commented.

"Yeah," Ferret chimed in. "The *tonton macoutes* who survived have all fled to parts unknown. We freed all the prisoners held in that damn tower, and helped them break into the storehouse so they could arm themselves. That guy named Jerry seems like he knows his business. He'll make a great new leader of the Resistance."

"Not that they need a Resistance anymore, no," Gremlin mentioned.

"All I care about is that Eleanore is doing okay," Lynx said. "A couple of days in bed and more food will have her back on her feet in no time."

Blade nodded. "All in all, a job well done. The people of New Orleans are free at last."

Lynx looked over his left shoulder at the temple, 40 yards to the southwest, and thought of the rotting carcass inside.

"I repeat. What the hell are we doing here?"

The giant was walking up a low mound. He halted on the crest and pointed. "We must dispose of them."

"Of what?" Lynx snapped testily, then stopped, astounded.

An immense circular depression lay on the other side, formed in the soft grass by the weight of a great body. Lying in the center of the nest were eighteen white eggs, each one a yard in length.

"I found this when I was out searching for a suitable branch to use as a spear," Blade related.

"Then this means Damballah was a she, yes?" Gremlin queried.

"Maybe. Maybe not," Blade replied.

"It means there's another one of those things out there somewhere," Ferret said, staring out over the bayou.

"And it's not our worry," Blade stated. "We've already proven Damballah wasn't a god. Jerry, Eleanore, and the rest will have to exterminate the mate if it ever shows up."

Lynx gestured at the nest. "Look. Can we get this over with and take off?"

"Something bothering you?" Ferret asked.

"Not a thing," Lynx answered, a tad nervously. "All the loose ends have been wrapped up."

Blade drew his Bowies. "Then let's get to it."

"Wait a minute," Lynx said.

"What?"

"There is one item I need cleared up. Have any of you guys ever heard about these geek octopuses—"